63
117

Boyfriends
WITH
GIRLFRIENDS

Boyfriends WITH GIRLFRIENDS

WITHDRAWN

Alex Sanchez

SIMON & SCHUSTER BFYR

NEW YORK   LONDON   TORONTO   SYDNEY

ALSO BY ALEX SANCHEZ

Bait

The God Box

Getting It

Rainbow Road

Rainbow High

Rainbow Boys

So Hard to Say

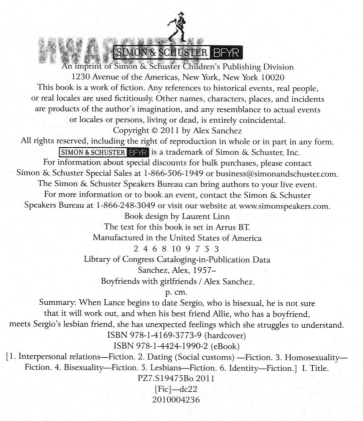

SIMON & SCHUSTER BFYR

An imprint of Simon & Schuster Children's Publishing Division
1230 Avenue of the Americas, New York, New York 10020
This book is a work of fiction. Any references to historical events, real people,
or real locales are used fictitiously. Other names, characters, places, and incidents
are products of the author's imagination, and any resemblance to actual events
or locales or persons, living or dead, is entirely coincidental.
SIMON & SCHUSTER BFYR is a trademark of Simon & Schuster, Inc.
For information about special discounts for bulk purchases, please contact
Simon & Schuster Special Sales at 1-866-506-1949 or business@simonandschuster.com.
The Simon & Schuster Speakers Bureau can bring authors to your live event.
For more information or to book an event, contact the Simon & Schuster
Speakers Bureau at 1-866-248-3049 or visit our website at www.simonspeakers.com.
Book design by Laurent Linn
The text for this book is set in Arrus BT.
Manufactured in the United States of America
2 4 6 8 10 9 7 5 3
Library of Congress Cataloging-in-Publication Data
Sanchez, Alex, 1957–
Boyfriends with girlfriends / Alex Sanchez.
p. cm.
Summary: When Lance begins to date Sergio, who is bisexual, he is not sure
that it will work out, and when his best friend Allie, who has a boyfriend,
meets Sergio's lesbian friend, she has unexpected feelings which she struggles to understand.
ISBN 978-1-4169-3773-9 (hardcover)
ISBN 978-1-4424-1990-2 (eBook)
[1. Interpersonal relations—Fiction. 2. Dating (Social customs) —Fiction. 3. Homosexuality—
Fiction. 4. Bisexuality—Fiction. 5. Lesbians—Fiction. 6. Identity—Fiction.] I. Title.
PZ7.S19475Bo 2011
[Fic]—dc22
2010004236

To those who dare to live label-free

ACKNOWLEDGMENTS

With gratitude to my editor, David Gale; my agent, Miriam Altshuler; assistant editor, Navah Wolfe; and all those who contributed to the creation of this book with their encouragement and feedback, including Bill and Jackie Hitz, Erica Lazaro, Tim Luscombe, John Porter, Dhamrongsak "Noom" Preechaboonyarit, John "J. Q." Quiñones, Nancy Schwartz, Pattawish Thitithanapak, and my inspiring typist, "Toast." Thank you all.

CHAPTER ONE

Lance tapped the beat of *A Chorus Line*'s "What I Did for Love" on Allie's bedroom door. "Hi, it's me!"

"Come in, you!" She opened the door in a jean skirt, adjusting her bra. Ambushed by her cleavage, Lance slapped a hand over his eyes.

"Oh, come on!" she giggled, holding up a tie-dyed T-shirt. "Help me decide! Should I go with the—"

He peeked through his fingers and cut her off: "No way!"

She lifted a zebra-stripe blouse. "How about the—"

"Ick!"

"Okay"—she held up a pink Lycra top—"I'll go with the—"

"Good!" He checked the time on his cell, eager to go meet the boy he'd friended online that week. "You think he'll like me?"

"He's going to go wild over you," she replied while pulling her blouse on.

"Wild is good." He put his arm around her and she snuggled up beside him in front of the mirror.

She'd always thought Lance was hot. At swim meets, when he strutted around the pool deck nearly naked, she'd often thought: *If he were straight or if I were a gay guy, I'd be all over him.*

"Feel something?" She planted a playful kiss on his cheek. "Anything?"

"Sorry." He began to hum a show tune, a nervous habit.

"From *My Fair Lady*," Allie said. "Right? What is it?"

He blushed, realizing what it was. "Why Can't a Woman Be More Like a Man?"

"Meanie!" She pulled away. "Shoes?"

"Your rose-color pointy pumps," he said, dabbing his blond hair with some of her gel.

"So, what did you say this guy's name is?" Allie asked as they climbed into Lance's car.

"Sergio," Lance said, pronouncing the *G* with an *H* sound. "He's Mexican. Hot and spicy!" Lance considered himself an equal opportunity dater, attracted to all types of guys—Latino, white, black, Asian. . . . He'd been attracted to Sergio's café latte–color skin, thick black hair gelled into spikes, eyes dark as night. And although his nose seemed kind of big, even that was cute. "He's a cousin of Penelope's from Drama Club."

The boys had gotten to know each other a little bit over the phone and Messenger. They were both seventeen. Sergio lived in a neighboring suburb and went to Liberty High.

"Home of the roaches," he'd joked. "Ew, yuck, right?"

Lance went to the Academy, a local private school. "But I'm not a big preppy or anything. I'm pretty down-to-earth."

"Good," Sergio replied. "Me too."

Sergio had an older sister in college; Lance was an only child. Sergio had a guinea pig named Elton; Lance had an Irish setter named Rufus.

"Help me think up stuff to talk about," he asked Allie as they drove toward the mall.

"Have you asked him what kind of movies he likes?" Allie suggested. "And what kind of music?"

"That's good," Lance said. "My main worry is the bi thing."

Sergio's "friend page" identified him as bisexual.

"I guess that means he's still coming out," Lance said to Allie. "Like in the saying: *bi now, gay later?* I just hope he's not another closet case."

He didn't want a repeat of Darrell, his one and only ex, who had been afraid to admit to being gay.

When Lance and Allie got to the mall, he hurried her toward the food court fountain and anxiously searched the crowd.

"Are you sure I look all right?"

"You look fab," Allie assured him, taking a seat on the fountain's rim. "So, who is the friend he's bringing?"

When setting up the meeting, Sergio had suggested they make it a friend thing. "You know, to take the pressure off?"

"She's his best chick friend," Lance said, taking a

seat beside Allie. "Her name is . . . Kimiko or something like that."

"Kimiko? Really? That's Japanese!" Allie was totally into anything Japanese.

It had been Kimiko who had given Sergio the initial kick in the butt to answer Lance's online friend request.

"Why *wouldn't* you friend him?" she'd asked Sergio when he showed her Lance's photos. "He looks gay-guy-adorable."

"Prezactly," Sergio had replied. "I'm not ready to get dumped again." He was still brokenhearted over Zelda; the girl who'd ditched him only three months earlier.

"You haven't even met the guy yet," Kimiko said, "and you're already worried about getting dumped?"

"Yeah, he's got that look: like someone who could be my future ex."

"Here's a thought." Kimiko bopped Sergio on the head. "Maybe he won't dump you."

"He won't if I don't meet him. *He he he.*" Nonetheless, Sergio had replied to Lance's friend request. And he'd enjoyed chatting with him.

"But what if there's no in-person chemistry?" Sergio now said as Kimiko prodded him through the food court toward the meeting. "Maybe he and I should just stick to communicating through electronic devices."

But when he saw Lance, there was chemistry, all right—both with Lance *and* his chick friend. *HE's a babe,* one part of Sergio thought while another part of him said, *Yeah, but SHE'S hot too!*

Luckily, he wasn't into tall girls—nor were they usually into him—whereas tall skinny guys like Lance juiced him up: broad swimmer shoulders, sweet smile, teacup-handle ears, and he loved the freckles.

"How do I look?" Sergio asked Kimiko. "No boogies hanging out my nose or anything?"

"You look good, dude." She tucked his flipped-up shirt tag into his collar and gazed toward Allie. "*That's his friend?*"

"Yeah, I guess so. She's a fox, huh?" Sergio knew that girlie-girls were totally Kimiko's type, even though she'd never actually been in a relationship.

"So . . . is she gay?" Kimiko asked—not that it made any difference; she had both gay and nongay friends. But she was curious.

"I don't know." Sergio gave her a mischievous grin. "I guess you get to find out."

"Well, do *I* look all right?" Kimiko asked, glancing down at her baggy boy's jeans and black leather motor-cycle jacket.

"Major league handsome." Sergio spun her Harley base-ball cap backward and took hold of her hand. "Come on!"

"There he is!" Lance told Allie on spotting him. "Curtain up!"

"Break a leg!" Allie whispered, standing beside him.

"What up, man? I'm Sergio. And this is Kimiko, my handler."

Everybody laughed and Lance asked, "Do you guys want to get smoothies?"

As they walked to the counter, he stealthily checked out Sergio. He was shorter than he had looked in his pictures—nice compact bod, hunky but not *too* buff, which was good. Excessive buffness intimidated Lance. He liked those pecs, though.

At the smoothie stand, he got his usual Hearty Apple. Sergio ordered a Mango Madness, took a sip—"Mmm"—and extended his cup to Lance. "Want a taste?"

"Um, okay." Lance stared at the straw that had touched Sergio's lips. "I've never tried mango before. I'm pretty plain-Jane. You want to try mine?"

"Sure." Sergio exchanged cups, watched Lance take a sip, and thought: *Damn, his freckles are hot!*

"Wow, that's *really* good." Lance handed the cup back, still tasting the sweet mango slush.

The girls led the way to a table while talking about mangas and other Japanese stuff. Allie sat beside Kimiko and Lance sat next to Sergio.

"So, um . . ." Lance began to ask the questions he'd rehearsed with Allie. "What kind of movies do you like?"

"Action!" Sergio replied, his hands slicing the air in a ninja move. "*Hooah!* . . . And fantasy-type stuff. How about you?"

"Disney 'toons . . . and chick flicks—nah, just kidding. Well, okay, sometimes. I admit it."

"Ditto!" Sergio high-fived him, glad that Lance was free of the straight-acting BS that so many other guys had.

"So, um, what kind of music do you like?" Lance continued.

"Different types," Sergio answered. "Trance . . . hip-hop . . . Tejano . . . How about you?"

"I'm huge on show tunes. Like I've got this kind of obnoxious habit of humming and singing showstoppers anytime, anywhere." He shuffled his feet. "Gotta sing! Gotta dance!"

"Glad you warned me." Sergio pretended to cover his ears, though in fact he liked Lance's voice: strong, smooth, sexy.

"Actually," Lance continued, "I'm a better singer than dancer."

"I'm just the opposite," Sergio said. "My singing sucks, but my dancing is pretty good—especially Latin stuff. I'm president of my school's Dance Club. Do you salsa? I can teach you."

"Cool!" Lance exclaimed. He'd always dreamed of dancing with a guy—holding him in his arms, moving together. . . . But first he needed to slow down, get back to the present. "So, um . . ." He moved to the next question on his list. "Are you out at school?"

"I'm out as bi," Sergio said, a little cautiously. Although girls usually accepted his bi-ness, with guys it sometimes seemed like the kiss of death.

The word *bi* prompted Allie to turn from her conversation with Kimiko and nod encouragingly to Lance.

"Well, um . . ." he stirred the slush in his smoothie cup and asked Sergio, ". . . what exactly do you mean when you say bi?"

"You know," Sergio said. "It means I'm turned on by both guys and chicks."

"But you admit you're attracted to guys?" Lance asked, trying not to come off as confrontational.

"Yeah . . . ," Sergio said. "But I'm also attracted to girls."

Lance chewed on his straw. At least Sergio was admitting he liked guys. That was a move up from Darrell. But why didn't he just take the next step and say he was gay? Maybe he wasn't as mature as Lance had hoped.

"Are *you* out at school?" Sergio asked, sipping his smoothie.

"Yeah. The Academy is pretty progressive. Allie and I started a GSA—you know—a Gay-Straight Alliance? I've never really gotten any flak. Have you?"

"Nothing major." Sergio shrugged. "I get called fag sometimes, but hey, doesn't everybody?"

"True," Lance agreed. He decided to drop the bi issue for now. *Maybe I'm making too big a deal of it.* He liked Sergio—his confidence, his coolness, and how his Adam's apple jutted out from his throat in a way that was ridiculously sexy. Plus, he noticed that Allie and Kimiko were getting along. *It would be awesome for them to become friends*, he thought, *so the four of us could do stuff . . . if Sergio and I became a couple.*

"What about your parents?" Sergio asked. "Do they know?"

"They knew before *me*!" Lance laughed and Sergio laughed too, relieved that they'd gotten over the bi bump.

"What about your family?" Lance asked. "Do they know about you?"

"Yeah. My blabbermouth older sis outed me. But my old man pretends like he doesn't know, and my mom prays I'll grow out of it. She lights novena candles, all that Latino Catholic mama drama."

Lance slurped the last of his smoothie, trying to recall what else he'd planned to ask. "So, um"—his voice went up—"are you seeing anyone?" Even though Sergio had said he was single on his page, Lance wanted to be sure.

"Nope," Sergio replied. "Not at the moment. Are you?"

"Um, no," Lance said, and glanced into his empty smoothie cup. He realized the only question he had remaining was the Big One: asking if Sergio wanted to go on a *real* date.

Sergio realized it too. Should he be the one to ask Lance out? It would be his first time to ask anyone out since Zelda. Was he ready to risk rejection again? Maybe he should wait, see if Lance asked. But what if Lance didn't ask?

He liked Lance. The dude was undeniably a hottie, even with his sticky-outy ears; he clearly had a mind; he wasn't stuck-up, despite going to private school; and it felt so refreshing to meet a guy his own age who was comfortable being out.

"So . . . ," Sergio ventured, " . . . do you want to go out sometime?"

Lance blinked. He hadn't expected Sergio to be the one to ask. He took a hard swallow, suddenly having second thoughts. Was he jumping into this too fast?

Across the table, Allie nodded for him to say yes.

"Sure," he told Sergio. "That would be great."

"Great," Sergio echoed and took a breath, both excited and nervous.

They returned to talking about simple stuff like favorite foods and books, each trying to relax, until Allie announced she needed to go—meaning that Lance had to go too.

Outside on the sidewalk, they all said good-bye and Allie took hold of Lance's arm as they walked back to his car.

"Look at you!" she whispered. "Mr. Got-Asked-for-a-Date-by-Hot-Sweet-Guy."

Lance forced a smile. It definitely had felt good to get asked out, but . . .

"Uh-oh," Allie said worriedly. "What's with the face?"

"The bi thing," Lance said as they climbed into his car. "I don't get it. He says he's attracted to guys; he's out at school; he asks me out on a date. And my state-of-the-art gaydar is ringing, *ding-ding-ding! Jackpot, he's gay!* So why can't he just say it?"

"I don't know." Allie stared across the car seat. "Maybe his parents are phobes and he's afraid they'll find out?"

"No, he said they know. His sister outed him."

"Then maybe he really is bi."

Lance frowned. "So where does that leave me?"

"Going out with a bi guy?" Allie replied.

"Lucky me," Lance mumbled and started the engine.

"But you were so excited," Allie said sadly.

"I know, I know! Let's see if he calls."

"You can call too," she encouraged him.

He backed out of the parking space, changing the subject. "Kimiko seems really cool. At first I wasn't sure if she was a girl or a guy—she's such a dude-chick with her cap and clothes. It seemed like you two got along great."

"Yeah, I'm so psyched she's Japanese. I wish we could've hung out longer."

From the sidewalk outside the mall, Kimiko watched Allie and Lance drive away, wishing they could've hung out longer too.

"Way to go, dude!" She turned to Sergio and fist-bumped him. "I overheard you ask him out."

Sergio bumped her fist in return. "So, what do you think of him?"

"I think he's the most perfecto guy in the world for you. He's your age, cute, gentle, nice. . . . What do *you* think of him?"

"I like him. I'm just not sure he gets the bi thing."

Kimiko's mouth drooped into a pout. "But you two seem good together."

"Yeah . . . Let's see if he calls. If not, I'll call him . . . in a couple of days."

"What are you afraid of?" Kimiko asked.

"I'm not afraid. That's just the rule with guys. Wait two days. . . . Otherwise I'll seem too easy."

Kimiko rolled her eyes; she'd heard his goofy theories and rules before.

"Now, as for you, girl—" he rested his arm on her

shoulder "—*you* should phone Allie ASAP. I could feel the mojo between you two all the way across the table."

"Dude, she's got a boyfriend."

"So?" Sergio persisted. "Maybe she's bi-curious."

"Even if she were . . ." Kimiko let out wistful breath. "She's out of my league."

"What're *you* afraid of?" Sergio asked, mimicking her.

"Shush!" Kimiko said and play-punched his arm.

CHAPTER TWO

When Kimiko had first seen Allie at the mall, she'd kind of stopped in her tracks, surprised by the über-girl with curly blond hair, a knockout figure, and an angel's face.

"'Sup?" Kimiko had said and boyishly fist-bumped her.

"Hi, I'm Allie—that's short for Alegría," she explained as they walked to the smoothie stand. "It's the Spanish word for 'joy.'"

"Sweet," Kimiko said. She immediately liked Allie's voice: breathy and femme. "My name is Japanese for 'noble child.' As if!"

"You *are* Japanese!" Allie's face lit up. "Oh my gosh! I'm an absolute Japan-geek—you wouldn't believe! My life dream is to go there. Have you been?"

"Yeah, like every summer. We go to visit my *obaasan*— that's my grandma."

"Can you write Japanese?" Allie asked when they got to a table. "Would you write something for me, please? Or is that too annoying?"

"No, it's okay." For the first time in her life, Kimiko actually felt grateful to her mom for the hours she'd made her spend learning Japanese. From her leather jacket, Kimiko pulled out the Sharpie pen and notepad she always carried to jot down notes for poems. "What would you like me to write?"

"Oh, anything. You decide."

Allie sipped her smoothie and Kimiko thought for a moment before writing.

"This is the word for 'joy,'" she said, tearing out the page and handing it to Allie. *"Yorokobi."*

"Awesome, thanks so much!" Allie exclaimed and held it out at arm's length, explaining, "I'm a little farsighted." She turned to Lance and Sergio. "Look! That's my name: Yorokobi."

"Cool," Lance said, admiring the kanji characters.

Kimiko already had a good feeling about him. He seemed easygoing, sweet, and good-natured.

Allie asked Kimiko her thoughts and opinions about all sorts of Japanese stuff: *Naruto*, J-pop, sushi, Hello Kitty, *Dragon Ball.* . . .

Kimiko had never met anybody her own age so interested in Japanese culture. She kind of liked being elevated to authority status. And she loved Allie's soft giggle.

"My fave manga are *shonen-ai*," Allie said. "You know: boy-boy love stories? Stuff like *Gravitation.* What kind do you like?"

"Shojo-ai, girls' love," Kimiko replied, hoping her reply might prompt Allie to reveal whether she was gay.

Allie had already assumed from Kimiko's guy clothes and square-shoulder stance that she was probably lesbian—maybe even transgender. "I've never read any girls' love," she told Kimiko. "You'll have to tell me your fave titles."

"I'd be glad to," Kimiko said, trying to figure Allie out—sexual orientation–wise.

As they continued to talk, Allie pulled out her cell phone and showed Kimiko her photos. "This is Lance and me in *Guys and Dolls* last year. . . . And this is my 'surprise' brother, Josh. . . ."

Kimiko tried to keep her attention on the pictures as Allie leaned closer, feeling comfortable, her shoulder unintentionally touching Kimiko's. She puckered her lips into a kiss at Josh's photo. . . . "This is my mom and dad . . . I'm a total Daddy's girl . . . and this is my boyfriend, Chip. . . ."

An unexpected sense of relief enveloped Kimiko: Allie was not only *not* lesbian; she was also taken—placing her safely out of bounds from the remotest possibility of their dating.

The boyfriend in the photos was WASPy all-American . . . tall . . . sandy-color hair . . . a ski-slope nose . . . everything the opposite of Kimiko.

"I've got to go meet him," Allie said, looking at the time. "Saturday is our date night." But she seemed like she didn't want to go, and neither did Kimiko. She was enjoying hanging out.

"How about you?" Allie asked. "Are you dating anyone?"

"Me?" Kimiko fidgeted with her cap, thinking: *My*

mom would never approve. Besides, who would I date? Who would want to date me?

"No," she told Allie. "No one."

"I find that hard to believe," Allie said with a smile, and Kimiko watched her eyes glisten—blue at first, then green, like the ocean.

"Would you like to hang out again sometime?" Allie asked.

"Huh? Sure," Kimiko said. She wasn't quite certain what to make of Allie. By all appearances she seemed like one of the cool kids—smart, good-looking, confident, no doubt popular—the type who usually brushed past Kimiko in the school hallway as if she didn't even exist. And yet she was asking Kimiko for her number and screen name.

While the girls exchanged info, Sergio gave Kimiko a suggestive grin—as if exchanging numbers meant something beyond becoming friends. She ignored him and put her phone away.

When the four of them finally wandered toward the exit, Allie kept stopping to check the window displays, and Kimiko definitely wasn't in a hurry either.

"Well," Allie said when at last they got outside. "Nice to meet you."

"Yeah, good to meet you, too," Kimiko replied, giving her a gentle fist-bump. Meeting Alice had felt *more* than good: kind of wonderful, actually. She liked Allie's unpretentiousness, considering how much she knew about Japanese stuff and how pretty she was; and she liked all the attention she'd gotten from Allie. It had felt *totally* wonderful, not just kind of.

After the mall, she went to Sergio's to hang out, listen to music, play a few games, and have dinner. His mom's spicy Mexican recipes were a welcome break from her own mom's delicate cooking, and she loved talking soccer with Sergio's dad. Plus, his parents were more lenient about them being alone together. Kimiko's mom wouldn't allow her to have a boy in her bedroom—as though there were the remotest need to worry. Kimiko had never felt even the slightest interest in guys as anything more than friends.

Later that night, she walked the three blocks home. Her parents were watching TV in the living room with her eight-year-old brother, Yukio, asleep on the sofa beside them.

"'Sup, I'm home," Kimiko announced and went to the kitchen for a glass of soy milk. Her mom followed shortly after her, bringing a tray with some rice cookies.

"Did you eat dinner?" she asked, setting the cookies next to Kimiko. "Here, have some. How was your day?"

"It was good, had dinner at Sergio's." She took a cookie and told her mom about meeting Lance and Allie, leaving out any allusion to anything gay. She was out and open at school and with friends, but not with her family—although surely they must know. *Just look at me,* she often thought. *How could they not know?*

"Sit like a lady, Miko." Her mom gently nudged Kimiko's knees together. "There, that's better."

Kimiko forced a smile and went along with it; she

wanted to be a good daughter. But in seconds, without her even realizing it, her knees again drifted apart like a boy's.

"This is my name in kanji." Allie showed the characters Kimiko had written to her boyfriend, Chip, during dinner. "Isn't it amazing?"

"Cool," he answered, giving the lettering a quick glance while grabbing another slice of their super-combo pizza. He'd never really gotten Allie's craziness for Japanese stuff. And with each passing day, Allie wondered if he really got *her*.

They'd been going out since freshman year, when she'd first spotted him towering over the hallway crowd. His height was a major selling point to a girl who constantly got flak for being tall. Even though she'd had several minor-league boyfriends, he'd become her first truly serious relationship. She liked his floppy hair, hazel eyes streaked with blue, and his gentle shyness. Unlike other boys, he didn't try to push himself on her, and when they kissed, he let her teach him how. Within a month after meeting, they'd become a couple: walking arm-in-arm in the hall, going to school dances together, bringing each other candy treats, telling each other, "I love you. . . ."

During tenth grade, they'd settled into each other, but over the last few weeks, as they returned to school for junior year, she'd begun to question their future together. Even though she still got sexually stoked by him, she no longer felt the same emotional connection. It felt as if they'd gone as far as they could go together and were drifting apart. She wanted to try something new, something different.

Tonight after dinner, they returned to the little bungalow behind his parents' house that he'd taken over as his band room, sat in their usual places on the sofa, and turned the TV on.

While he surfed through channels, she debated how to talk to him about her doubts. Maybe she should just hold on and wait till graduation. Then they'd go away to separate colleges and she'd have more space to figure out her feelings—except that was nearly two years away.

After settling on a music video program, he leaned across the couch to kiss her and she went along for a moment. Then she pulled away.

"How do you feel about our relationship?"

"Um . . ." His brow crinkled as he leaned back, obviously surprised. "Good . . . Why? What's the matter? Did I do something wrong?"

"No, no, no." She didn't blame him for anything. He was the same person he'd always been. "It's just . . . Where do you think our relationship is going?"

"I don't know." His face went blank. "I haven't really thought about it. . . . I guess we'd finish school . . . go to college together . . . see what happens. Why? What do *you* think is our future?"

"I'm not sure," Allie said. She became quiet, and they stared at each other. She wasn't sure what else to say at this point.

"Well," he said at last, "the important thing is that I love you."

Hearing that failed to resolve her uncertainty; instead it sort of made her feel guilty.

"I love you, too," she answered. But saying it didn't feel the same as it used to.

He bent over again to kiss her again, and she knew that unless she stopped things, they'd soon be shedding clothes and putting the condom on.

"Do you mind if we just make out tonight?" she asked.

He peered at her a moment, looking a little wounded. "Um, okay. Are you sure everything is all right?"

"Yeah, I'm just in a weird mood," she replied. "Sorry." She leaned across and kissed him, even though she wasn't feeling exactly thrilled.

While they made out, her mind began to drift . . . first to Kimiko and how much she'd liked hanging out with her . . . then to the Academy's tiny six-person Gay-Straight Alliance . . . and how, although Chip had never said anything against her participating in the club, he'd never shown any interest in going to meetings. . . . He'd never really gotten that aspect of her either.

After making out for a while, they just held each other, watching and listening to the music videos. She liked holding him and being held by him. And for a moment, the feeling of connection returned.

On her drive home, she put in her earphone and called Lance to check in. "Hey, babe. How's it going?"

"Um, okay." He was in the middle of peeling off his

clothes, getting ready for bed. "I ended up going to eat veggie food with Megan and Nancy." They were two friends of theirs from the school GSA club. "And you?" he asked Allie. "How did it go with the Chip-meister?"

"I want to ask you something," Allie answered. "Do you think I'm, like, settling with him?"

"Um, I don't know." Although she'd hinted to Lance about her doubts before, the question took him by surprise. "Do *you* think you're settling?"

"I don't know either." She stopped at a traffic light. "I think he's a great guy. I mean, in the two years we've gone out, he's never lied or cheated on me. He doesn't do drugs. . . . He's good-hearted and generous. . . . Plus, I still think he's hot. So why don't I feel excited about him anymore?"

Lance lay down in bed, trying to think of an answer. "Maybe that's just what happens after you've gone out with somebody for a couple of years." Then he added: "Wow, that's depressing."

"I still feel excited to see *you* every day," Allie argued. "And I've known you for—what—ten years?"

Lance shifted his phone from one ear to the other, as a familiar worry popped up: Had she grown too attached to him?

Once at a party, she'd gotten kind of drunkish and when he drove her home she'd cooed, "You're my hero, you know that? My best friend, my soul mate"—a hiccup interrupted her—"oops, sorry." She covered her mouth, then began again: "I'm a better person because of you. I doubt I'll ever love anybody as much as I love you."

"I love you, too," he'd told her, even though he felt nervous she might be putting the make on him. But she hadn't, and the next day she'd apologized for being "kind of a mess last night."

"Maybe you should just be honest with him," Lance now suggested. "Tell him how you feel."

"I don't want to hurt him," Allie said, turning onto her street. "Besides, I'm not sure how I feel. I mean, even though I don't feel like he *completes* me or anything like that, I still care about him. You know what I mean? I feel comfortable and safe with him. Shouldn't that be enough? Maybe I'm expecting too much. But if I'm *not* in love with him anymore, am I like misleading him?"

"You're not in love with him anymore?" Lance asked. It was the first time he'd heard that from her.

"I don't know. On some days I wonder if I ever *was* in love with him. Maybe it was just infatuation. But then I wonder if maybe it's not really about him; maybe it's about me. I mean: Maybe there's more to me I still want to explore."

"That's cool," Lance said. "Like what?"

"I'm not sure." She gave a long, questioning sigh as she pulled into her driveway. "Anyway, thanks for listening."

"Sure, anytime." It was apparent she'd gone as far as she wanted to go with the topic for now.

When she got into her house, her mom and dad were watching *Saturday Night Live*. She sat with them for a while, and on the way to her room she peeked in on Josh and watched him sleeping.

Inside her room, she pulled Kimiko's kanji out from her bag. And as she undressed and got ready for bed, she recalled times growing up when she'd met a new girl and become friends; and how she'd felt a sort of crush, thinking how pretty the girl looked and how much she liked to be with her. The feelings had eventually died down, and she'd never thought of them as romantic or sexual.

But there was one night in middle school, when she dreamed she had sex with a girl, and the next morning she woke up with her whole body tingling. The experience had felt as intense as any sex dream she'd ever had about a boy.

On the school bus she'd told Lance about the dream, giggling nervously.

"You're gay!" he whispered, thrilled to think his best friend since first grade was a latent lesbian.

"You really think so?" Allie stared out the window, thinking about it. "But then why do I get turned on by guys? Lesbians don't, do they? Maybe I'm bi."

"I think bi's kind of a cop-out," Lance argued. "Maybe you should try it with a girl—I mean, at least try kissing or something."

"With who?" Allie asked. She felt too chicken to do anything with any girl from her school or church. No way. Nevertheless, she did mention the dream to her friend Jenny, after field hockey practice one day—or at least she tried to.

"I've got a question for you," she said in a low voice. "Have you ever had a sex dream about . . . a girl?"

"No!" Jenny scrunched up her face in disapproval. "That's gay! Why? Did you?"

"No," Allie lied, regretting having asked. "I was just curious."

"I mean," Jenny said, softening her tone. "I like Lance and I've got nothing against gay people, but that doesn't mean I'm gay. So why would I ever have a sex dream about a girl?"

"I don't know," Allie said, and quickly changed the subject.

After that experience, she'd put the dream aside, and never had another like it. And as she began to date boys, she'd almost completely forgotten about the dream. Now, as she pinned the kanji up on the bulletin board above her computer, she remembered the dream for an instant and thought how cool it was going to be to have Kimiko as a friend.

On Sunday morning when Lance's alarm rang, he mistakenly grabbed his cell phone instead, groggily hoping it was Sergio calling. Realizing it wasn't, he shut off the alarm and lay thinking for a moment, recalling Sergio's hunky pecs. . . .

Maybe I'm making too much of the bi thing, he thought as he tumbled out of bed and shuffled toward the shower, taking his phone along—just in case.

His dad made breakfast: turkey bacon and French toast. Lance squirted maple syrup into his glass of milk: his comfort bev.

"Expecting a call, honey?" his mom asked, as he stared at his phone on the kitchen table.

Lance shrugged, not wanting to go into it with her—even though his mom and dad were completely cool with him being gay.

The first time the issue had come up, he'd been barely eight years old. A TV news story about commitment ceremonies showed a pair of guys in tuxes hugging and laughing as they cut a wedding cake topped with two little groom figurines.

"When I grow up," Lance had announced to his parents, "I want to marry a man."

His mom peered at him a moment, then turned to his dad.

"Well"—his dad stared back at her—"I guess you were right."

"Right about what?" Lance asked.

After an awkward silence, his dad told his mom, "This one is all yours. Go for it!"

"Gee, thanks." His mom smirked and turned to Lance. "Well, honey . . . Right about . . . that you might want to make a family with a man someday . . . And if that's what you want, well . . . that's okay. The important thing is Daddy and I love you very much. That's all that matters."

Lance returned to watching the tuxedoed men on TV, not really understanding what had just happened, but feeling happy.

With Allie, too, his coming out had been pretty much unnecessary. In grade school, they'd played Barbies at her house while they giggled about which boys in class were cutest.

In middle school, when other boys traded drawings of girls' boobs, Lance didn't get the point. He loved to be with Allie, but he felt no desire to see her—or any other girl—naked.

When classmates began to use words like *homo* and *queer* about people, Lance started to put all the pieces together. But he didn't think it was a big deal until one day in seventh grade when a girl asked him point-blank, "Are you gay?"

"Yeah, I guess." It was his first time to admit it out loud.

By day's end, the entire school was buzzing with the news. Nobody really hassled him; people were mostly just curious. But since he'd never actually had sex with anybody, he didn't have much to tell. Within a week, kids lost interest; he never really had to deal with any homophobes.

High school brought a couple of small-time boyfriends, culminating with the Big One: Darrell Wright, a JV point guard that all the girls crushed on. So did Lance. But he never seriously imagined he stood a chance with him . . . until one afternoon.

He was heading home from Drama Club, Darrell was leaving basketball practice, and they found themselves alone in the boys' restroom.

"So, like, is it true what people say about you?" Darrell asked.

Lance braced himself, a little nervous. "Um, yeah."

Darrell glanced warily toward the door and whispered, "You want to come over?"

When they got to his house, Darrell unloaded an avalanche of questions: How had Lance known he was gay? Did he think he could change? Did his parents suspect? Had he ever done anything with a guy?

Lance answered everything honestly, although uncertain where all this was headed. Then Darrell turned silent, giving him an odd look of anticipation. A heartbeat later, they were feverishly running their hands all over each other—across shirts and down jeans. It was the closest

Lance had ever come to sex. And just as suddenly, Darrell pulled away.

"My parents are home!"

Lance became aware of a car engine turning off outside, doors opening and closing.

"Try not to act gay!" Darrell told him.

"But I am gay," Lance said in a low voice.

"Just try!" Darrell insisted. *"Please?"*

Lance tried his best not to "act gay," whatever that meant, as he met Darrell's dad, a glum, unsmiling man, and his mom, an equally stern-looking woman.

"Don't tell anyone about this, okay?" Darrell whispered as he walked Lance outside.

"Okay," Lance agreed, feeling a little dazed. This wasn't how he'd imagined his first sexual experience. Shouldn't he feel like singing as in some musical—or at least humming?

He *had* to tell somebody about it. As always, that someone was Allie.

"Darrell Wright is *gay*?" She giggled and gasped. "No way!"

"Way," Lance replied. "And he kind of said I act gay. Do you think I do? Come on. Tell me. Be honest."

"Well . . ." Allie hesitated, not sure how he'd take it. " . . . Maybe, sometimes, a little."

He perched his hands on his hips and rolled his eyes. "I didn't mean *that* honest!"

"See?" she said. "Like when you stand like that and roll your eyes."

"Why, what's wrong with how I'm standing?"

"Nothing is *wrong* with it; it's just not something most straight guys do."

"Okay." He crossed his arms. "I'll stop doing it."

"Babe, you shouldn't change who you are just to please Darrell. Maybe you should just wait for a different guy."

But it was too late: Lance had already begun to fall for Darrell. Hard. Head-over-sneakers hard. Harder than he'd ever crushed on any boy.

At school, Darrell avoided any acknowledgment of him beyond, "'Sup?"

Nevertheless, Lance invited him to sit at his group's table.

"Thanks," Darrell said. "But I don't want people to get ideas."

"Um, *what* ideas?"

"About us . . . Look, you can be whatever you want, but . . . I can't."

"Yes, you can. Just come out!"

"I can't," Darrell insisted, and the next time they were together, he explained, "My parents would disown me. Besides, I still want to get married and have kids someday."

"You can do that with a guy," Lance argued.

"Not with my family." Darrell gave a hopeless sigh. "And even if I could, it wouldn't be the same."

"But if you're gay, you're gay," Lance persisted.

"I'm not sure I'm gay," Darrell said, despite having had

his hands inside Lance's pants. "I'm not going to come out."

And yet every few days he once again waited for Lance after school.

When they were apart, Lance phoned, e-mailed, and texted him constantly: *Where r u? Miss u.* And an hour later: *Sup? What r u doing now?* When asleep, he even dreamed about him. He couldn't get Darrell out of his mind. He loved his foresty smell, his dark-dark skin, his gleaming white smile. He ached to do everything with him, spend every moment together.

"I can't help feeling kind of sorry for him," Lance explained to Allie. "I'm the only person he's really open to. Maybe with time, he'll change and accept he's gay."

"Are you sure about this?" Allie asked.

"No," Lance admitted, "but I'm sure I love him."

Nonetheless, as the days passed Darrell and he got into more and more arguments, mostly about the closety sneaking around and Darrell's not wanting to be seen with him in public. And yet Lance couldn't give him up. Instead he decided to try harder. Maybe if he told Darrell how he really felt, then Darrell would change and come out.

"I love you," Lance finally told him one afternoon. His pulse beat wildly while he waited for Darrell to say it back. . . . But Darrell didn't.

"I can't do this anymore," Darrell said and turned away.

Lance's heart sank like a stone.

"What did I do wrong?" he asked Allie over the phone afterward. "I only want to love him."

"You didn't do anything wrong," Allie consoled him. "It's not about you. But maybe you should ease up on him. Give him some space."

Lance cut back on texts and IMs. But even so, Darrell no longer waited for him after school. And he stopped answering Lance's calls—until after about the hundredth time, when Darrell finally told him, "Don't call me again, okay?"

It cut like a knife to see Darrell every day at school and be ignored. For weeks, Lance stumbled around with a hollow emptiness inside his chest, feeling as though his life was over; he might as well just lie down and die.

"Brace yourself," Allie told him one day in the hall. "I just heard Darrell is going with Fiona."

"He's going out with a *girl*?" Lance asked. He leaned back onto his locker in disbelief, unsure whether to feel hurt or angry or even more sorry for him. On one hand, he wanted to expose Darrell as a fake who liked to stick his tongue in another boy's ear; on the other hand, he felt kind of sorry for Darrell, wanted to cradle him in his arms and tell him, "Dude, you don't have to pretend. Just be yourself."

"What should I do?" he asked Allie.

"I think you should just let the whole thing go," she suggested.

Gradually, Lance tried to date other guys. But it seemed as though they were either too young and imma- ture, too old and bossy, didn't have time for him, lived too far across the city, already had a relationship, weren't into him, or only wanted sex. . . . Not that he had anything against sex. He liked sex—at least the little bit of it he'd had.

"Is it *me*?" he asked Allie. "Why is it so hard to find a guy to love? I'm seventeen already! I should have a boyfriend by now. I'm not a bad person, am I? What's wrong with me?"

"Nothing is wrong with you," Allie reassured him. "Take it easy. You'll find someone."

He hoped she was right. At least *she'd* always love him, even if nobody else ever did.

The evening after meeting Sergio, Lance went online and surfed through his friends' friend lists—the same way he'd initially found Sergio. But no one caught his attention and he returned to Sergio's page.

When he'd first read the page, he'd liked how out and open Sergio sounded, not caring what anybody thought of him—the total opposite of Darrell.

Sergio's page included a Helen Keller quote: *"Life is either a daring adventure or nothing." That's me,* Sergio wrote, *daring and dramatic, provocative and controversial. Hola!*

Okay, Lance now thought, *so then why don't you just admit you're gay?*

On impulse, he picked up the phone to call him, but then stopped himself. He wasn't ready to risk it.

A little before noon on that Sunday after meeting Lance, Sergio woke up and checked his cell. It surprised him that

Lance hadn't called or texted. The dude had seemed so puppy-dog eager. He set the phone down and lay beneath the warm and toasty sheets, thinking about Lance's yummy white skin speckled with freckles. . . . And within seconds he was into a full-blown fantasy, with Lance snuggled beside him.

I hope I locked the door, Sergio thought.

One time his mom had walked in on him solo-sexing. Whoops! *Mortifying*. That night she took his sister out shopping so his dad could give him the Talk.

His old man had paced the living room carpet, jingling a pocket full of coins and clearing his throat—"ahem . . ."—while lecturing Sergio about the perils of girls and "canoodling."

What the hell kind of word is that? Sergio wondered.

Above all, his dad emphasized the importance of good hygiene—as if being extra clean was the most significant part of sex. And he never even broached the possibility that Sergio might be attracted to *guys* as well as girls.

Since at least kindergarten, Sergio had liked both— playing "doctor" with the boy next door; kissing girls during Spin the Bottle; and smooching in the restroom with a kid named Peter.

Guys and girls brought out different feelings in him. With boys, he liked the rough-and-tumble play, their earthy smells and no-nonsense talk, the fact that in so many ways they were the same as he was. With girls he liked everything the opposite: their soft tender touch, their flowery scents, the way they flirted and teased, their difference and mystery. By the time he'd finished grade school, he'd scored kisses from three boys and three girls. The teams were tied, even-steven.

When he reached middle school, his antsy hormones began to demand more excitement, and he discovered that to get any action from a girl required a lot more preliminaries. First, a friend had to tell the girl that Sergio liked her. If she liked him back, he'd need to talk on the phone and IM her for hours, telling her *how much* he liked her . . . until finally, he might get a kiss. And if he got super-lucky she'd let him sneak a little feel.

Fooling around with boys was way less complicated. They could wrestle and horse around, and if a hand strayed below the waist, they just giggled about it and punched each other.

With middle school also came porn. One afternoon in seventh grade, his buddy, Big Brian, showed him how to get around his computer's Net Nanny, and they pornsurfed, stumbling onto an all-male site.

"They're gay," Sergio said, stating the obvious.

"Yeah, gross," Brian said. But he didn't change the page.

"Um . . ." Sergio squirmed, staring at the pictures. " . . . You ever wondered what that would feel like?"

"Nah." Brian's voice quivered in response. "Have you?"

Sergio shrugged evasively. "You want to try it?"

"Um . . ." Beads of sweat broke out on Brian's forehead. "You want?"

Their belts got unbuckled fast; pants fumbled open.

"You go first," Brian whispered.

"But how do you . . . ?" The boys studied the photos, trying to figure things out.

"Oh, I get it. Like this!"

"Man, that feels great."

"Yeah!" Hearts pounded among echoes of "Yeah! Yeah!"

Afterward, they cleaned up with a crusty old sock, grabbed chips and soda from the kitchen, played a computer game, and the next day went to school like any other seventh-grade boys. They never talked about their experiences; it was easier not to.

In high school Sergio began to date, alternating between guys and girls, until he met Zelda, his first serious relationship.

He was sitting one day between the school library shelves reading *A Wizard of Earthsea*, when a girl's voice whispered, "Hey, that's the book I was looking for."

He gazed up a pair of long slender Lycra-panted legs at an impish-looking girl with a butterfly sticker on her cheek.

"How is it?" Zelda asked, pushing her raven black hair behind her ears. "My friend tells me it's great."

"Yeah," he replied. "It's my second time reading it."

She plopped down onto the carpet beside him, where they talked about their favorite fantasy books, and then about time travel, and then about trance music. . . . When the end-of-period bell rang, he knew he wanted to spend more time with her.

"I'll let you take the book," he teased, "if you give me your number."

She smiled, but only a little—as if she didn't want him to think he was getting too big a bargain—and wrote her number on his hand.

Within a week, they were talking on the phone every day—about school, their families, favorite foods, anything and everything. . . . He opened up to her more than he'd ever opened up to anyone except Kimiko.

"Just so you know, I'm bi," he told Zelda, wanting to be honest. But in reality he'd stopped thinking about guys. She'd become the only person he thought about—almost each and every moment.

"I'm bi too sometimes," she said with a half smile.

"Sweet!" he replied, feeling he could be totally himself with her.

He loved the time they spent together . . . talking, kissing, holding. . . . He loved everything about her: when her hair fell across her forehead and how silky soft it felt when he combed his fingers through it; how her breasts fit into his cupped hands like two golden apples—the first bare boobs he'd ever touched; how their bodies seemed to fit together perfectly; he loved her body naked, damp and moist after they'd made full-on love. It all seemed so cosmic. . . .

Until the afternoon Kimiko came over, acting weird and evasive—fidgeting, not looking him in the eye.

"What's up with you today?" he asked.

"I saw Zelda at the mall . . . ," she muttered softly, ". . . with some guy. I've never seen him at school."

"So?" Sergio felt his chest tighten. "The guy was probably her cousin or something."

"Dude, the guy didn't exactly look like a relative. He was black. Zelda is white. And . . . they were holding hands."

Sergio felt his head grow warm. "I don't believe you."

"Why would I lie to you?" Kimiko asked.

He knew she wouldn't, but he didn't want to believe her.

"Maybe you'd better ask her about him," Kimiko suggested.

After she left, he played Tetris on his phone for a while, trying to ignore what she'd said, until he finally shut the game down. He dialed Zelda's number, counting the number of rings: one . . . two . . . three . . . fo—

"Hi," she answered, just like normal. Obviously, Kimiko had been wrong.

They talked for a few minutes about nothing impor-tant, while Sergio debated whether to mention what Kimiko had told him.

"I heard you were at the mall this afternoon," he said at last.

Zelda suddenly went quiet—only for a moment, but long enough for Sergio to notice.

"Yeah," she replied. "I went with a friend."

"Who?" Sergio asked, scooting back on his bed against the headboard.

"A friend," Zelda repeated. Her voice seemed tense. " . . . Why?"

Sergio grabbed a pillow and clutched it to his chest. "Because you two were holding hands."

Zelda let out a loud sigh. "Look, this isn't working for me."

"*What* isn't working for you?"

"*This.* Us. I'm always wondering: Are you thinking about me or about a guy?"

Her comment took Sergio by surprise. "Why would you wonder that?"

"Because you're bi! Whenever we're kissing or anything, I never know if you're really thinking about me or about some guy."

"If I wanted to be with a guy," Sergio replied, "I'd be with a guy. I'm with you because I want to be with you."

She turned quiet again as though contemplating what he'd said. "I just don't think this can work. I don't want to be a couple anymore."

"But why?" He clutched the pillow more tightly to his chest.

"Because you're gay."

"I'm not gay; I'm *bi*. If I was gay I wouldn't have sex with you, would I?"

On the other end of the line, she took a breath. "I don't like how you're talking to me."

"How do you expect me to talk? *You're* the one who's cheating on me with another guy. I told you I was bi from the start. If you had a problem with it, you should've said so. Why are you trying to blame this on me?"

The phone line clicked off.

"Hello?" he demanded and started to call her back, but then he stopped himself. What would be the point?

"You bitch!" He hurled the phone onto the mattress but it bounced to the floor. "Shit!" He sprang off the bed and grabbed the cell. Seeing that it was okay, he speed-dialed Kimiko.

"You were right," he told her, his voice quivering. "I'm sorry I doubted you. She dumped me."

"Hang on," she told him. "I'll be right over."

"I'm so pissed at her," he told Kimiko when she arrived. "And at *myself*. Why did I trust her? I was so stupid! Why did I ever go out with her?"

"Because you were in love . . . Here . . ." She handed him a pillow to punch. "Give it a whack."

He punched the pillow several times. Then the tears began to flow. Kimiko put her arm around him while he sobbed and wiped his nose, until his tear ducts hurt.

In the months since the breakup, he'd tried to numb his hurt feelings in any way he could: eating chocolates by the carton, working out, hooking up with guys over the Internet, wasting hours trying to teach tricks to his guinea pig.

"'Sup, watch," he told Kimiko when she came over. "Come on, Elton! Stand up! " He held a food pellet above its head. "He did it this morning. I think he's nervous that you're watching him."

"Dude," Kimiko said, "you need to get a life."

"I have a life," he muttered. "Come on, Elton! You can do it."

But he knew deep down that she was right. After a while, he got tired of hooking up. Some of the guys he'd met were so cold and impersonal that they left him feeling like a slab of meat. Others were so scared and jumpy that it was hard to have much fun at all.

He wanted a real relationship, someone he could talk with, do stuff together with, teach and learn from. . . . Yet at the same time he wondered: Would—*could*—he ever fall in love again? He'd gradually gotten over Zelda, but the experience had left him with a lingering sense of mistrust.

"Have you called Lance?" Kimiko asked him at school.

"No," Sergio muttered. "He hasn't called me either. I think it's because of the bi thing. If he can't deal with it, I don't want to push it."

"Well, then maybe you should give Serena a chance," Kimiko suggested, referring to the new girl in her creative writing class. "She asked me if you're going out with anyone. She's cute, smart, and has a nice rack."

It cracked Sergio up when Kimiko guy-talked like that.

"Did you tell her I'm bi?" he asked.

"Yeah. She seems cool with it."

For a minute Sergio considered the idea of going out with Serena. "But every time I think about a girl, I'm reminded of Zelda."

"Then maybe," Kimiko said, "you're not ready for a relationship again."

"Maybe," he agreed. But after school that day, he returned to Lance's online photos. The one that most snagged his attention was an abs shot in which Lance shyly lifted his shirt to reveal six neatly stacked little white bricks.

"Screw it!" he said suddenly and dialed Lance's number. It hadn't been two days yet, but he no longer cared. He'd always sucked at rules anyway.

CHAPTER FOUR

"He called!" Lance announced when Allie answered her phone. "We're meeting up Saturday for dinner and a movie—just the two of us."

"Woo-hoo!" Allie cheered, breaking from the calculus she'd been working on.

"Yeah, I'm kind of psyched," Lance said. "Actually, I'm *really* psyched." He paced his bedroom, unable to sit still. "Can you like come pull me off the ceiling?"

Hearing Lance's excitement made Allie think about her own *lack* of excitement with Chip. She missed that thrilling sense of possibility she'd once felt with him.

After talking with Lance, she finished her homework and went online. In her in-box she found an e-mail from her school anime and manga club reminding her about a convention coming up Saturday.

She glanced up at the kanji lettering on her bulletin board. Would Kimiko want to go with her?

Kimiko had just come home with her little brother from their karate classes when her cell rang. Allie's name appeared on the screen. Kimiko's heart went into a gallop as she answered, "'Sup?"

"Hi, this is Allie. Remember me?"

"Dude, of course," Kimiko replied, bounding upstairs to her room. "From the mall, right?"

"Right," Allie said, moving to the loveseat across her bedroom. "What are you up to?"

"Not much." Kimiko closed her door. "Just came home from karate with my little bro."

"Karate?" Allie asked. "Wow, that's so cool! How long have you been doing that?"

"Since I was six," Kimiko said modestly. Even though she'd progressed to brown belt, the second highest *kyu* level, her family had taught her not to boast. One of her mom's constant admonitions was: "The nail that sticks out gets hammered down."

"Do you play any sports?" Kimiko asked Allie.

"Bowling, swimming, tennis . . . nothing like karate. I'm impressed."

"No big deal," Kimiko said, picturing Allie in a cute white tennis outfit.

"So, did you ever wish you lived in Japan instead of the U.S.?" Allie asked.

"No, I'm definitely American," Kimiko said and sat down on the rug. "Though it might've been easier to grow up there. Here I got picked on by kids saying stuff like: 'Your eyes are weird,' or 'Where's your nose?'"

"I wish *I* had your nose," Allie replied. "I've never liked mine."

"Are you kidding?" Kimiko said, recalling Allie's ski-jump nose. "Your nose is beautiful, dude."

"Thanks!" Allie laughed. Nobody had ever complimented her nose before. "I think your eyes are beautiful."

Kimiko turned quiet. Was Allie flirting with her? *Yeah, right,* she told herself. *Keep dreaming!*

"I guess we all get picked on for something," Allie continued. "I got the tall jokes: 'How is the weather up there? Har-har-har.' *So* annoying."

"Dude, I wish *I* were as tall as you. I got called shrimp."

"Well, I wish I were petite like you."

"Petite?" That sounded daintier than Kimiko thought of herself. "Not me! I remember one time in kindergarten I got so mad at this boy teasing me that I slugged him in the stomach."

"Really?" Allie giggled.

"Yeah. My mom was like horrified. That's when my dad sent me to karate to teach me self-control. I think he always wished I'd been born a boy. I did too."

"You did?" Allie asked. She'd wondered at times if gay people wished they were the opposite sex. "I asked Lance if he'd ever wanted to be a girl, and he told me, 'Never! I like being a guy.'"

"Yeah, who wouldn't want to be a guy?" Kimiko said and glanced at herself in the mirror: boy's jeans, oversize T-shirt, baseball cap. "Guys get all the breaks."

"Well, I'm glad I'm a girl," Allie replied. "I never wanted to be a guy. So, do you consider yourself trans?"

"No, just butch. I never wanted to get a sex change, or

felt I was born in the wrong body, or anything like that. But if somebody mistakes me for a guy, that's cool. I wish people wouldn't get so hung up on gender. You know?"

"Well, last year"—Allie giggled—"for Halloween I borrowed one of my dad's suits and I wore a fake mustache? It was such a hoot! But you could still tell I was a girl."

"I would've loved to see that." Kimiko laughed, trying to picture it in her mind.

"I'll e-mail you a photo," Allie said, returning to her computer. "Hey, would you like to go to a manga convention Saturday afternoon?"

"Dude, I'd love to!" Kimiko pumped her fist in the air, excited.

"Super," Allie said. "I'll pick you up so we can go together."

They continued to talk for another half hour while Kimiko stared at the JPEG Allie sent of herself in guy drag. Although the picture was cute, Kimiko definitely liked her better as a girl.

After hanging up, Kimiko immediately phoned Sergio and told him about the call.

"Kimiko's got a date," he teased in singsong. "Kimiko's got a date!"

"You're being a dork," Kimiko replied. "We're just going as friends. It's not a date"—although she wished it were.

On Friday evening, she went over to Sergio's for dinner. Afterward, they hung out in his room, listening to music while he debated what to wear for his date with Lance the following night.

"Do you think he's a virgin?" Sergio asked as he picked through shirts. "He kind of gives off that vibe like: 'I want you to seduce me.' Did you notice?"

Kimiko gave him a look as though to say: *Are you insane?*

"Since it's your first date," she suggested, "maybe you guys should go slow—stick to just making out and get to know each other first."

Sergio gave her a grumpy pout and put on a red shirt with buttons down the front. "How about this one? Good for easy access! *He he he.*"

"When did you get that?" Kimiko said, admiring the shirt. "Can I borrow it sometime?" Even when she was little she'd worn clothes from the boys' section.

"But you're a *girl*!" her mom had argued, trying to entice her with ruffled skirts and frilly blouses, to no avail.

"You want to wear it tomorrow?" Sergio asked, pulling the shirt off. "On your date with Allie?"

"Dude, you're really getting annoying. Pick something else out for me."

"Here, you always liked this one," Sergio said, pulling out a western cowboy shirt with curlicue stitching. As Kimiko put it on, Sergio gazed at her in the mirror. "You look awesome in it, though maybe you should ditch the baseball cap? Otherwise you two will look like dipstick and lipstick." He pulled her cap off and tossed it onto the bed. Then he combed his fingers through her hat hair. "Let her see your eyes!"

"She said she thinks they're beautiful," Kimiko whispered.

"But it's not a date, huh?"

"It's *not*! Girls say that kind of stuff to each other all the time. It doesn't mean anything."

"Riiight," he said and rested his chin on her shoulder.

After showering on Saturday morning, Kimiko put on the borrowed cowboy shirt but couldn't bring herself to abandon the baseball cap. Even if it did hide her eyes, without it she felt naked. Instead, she spun the bill around backward, like Sergio always did.

When the doorbell rang after lunch, she raced downstairs. On the front stoop stood Allie, wearing a hair band with little velour cat's ears. Thick black eyeliner framed her eyes, sixties style. And she wore a pair of low, low, *low-*rise skinny jeans.

Kimiko drew in a breath. *Oh. My. Goddess.*

"'Sup, dude?" She fist-bumped Allie and explained her family's shoe custom: "You leave them facing the door and change into house slippers."

As Allie turned around, Kimiko couldn't help notice the top rear thong strap—it peeked above Allie's waistline like a whale's tail rising gracefully out of the ocean.

Kimiko steadied herself and led Allie to the living room. "Come meet my family!"

Although her dad wasn't usually a big smiler, upon meeting Allie he couldn't stop grinning. And her little brother, who generally ignored Kimiko's friends, showed Allie his latest handheld game.

What happened to my REAL dad and brother? Kimiko wondered.

"Please, sit down," her mom told Allie and complimented

Allie's pink sweater set. "It's lovely. . . . Isn't it, Miko? Why don't you wear something like that?"

Kimiko didn't bother to answer.

Allie felt thrilled to be meeting a real-life Japanese family. "My dream is to go to Japan," she told Kimiko's mom.

"You should go," Mrs. Kawabata said, serving them chrysanthemum ice tea.

A wild idea popped into Kimiko's mind: *Maybe she could come with us next summer!* Then she noticed her mom signaling her about how she was sitting. Dutifully, she brought her knees together.

"I like your family," Allie said as she and Kimiko walked outside.

"They're okay," Kimiko agreed. If only her mom would accept her more.

Allie unlocked her car—a VW bug with a daisy in the little dashboard vase.

"Sweet!" Kimiko exclaimed, brushing her fingertips across the velvety petals. "I love flowers."

"Me too," Allie said, plugging in her iPod and handing it to Kimiko. "Here, you want to choose something? What do you like? I've got lots of J-pop."

"I'm not really a big J-pop fan," Kimiko said, but she saw that Allie had a lot of sixties rock and roll, which Kimiko liked. As they drove along, she picked out a Beatles playlist, and when Allie began to sing along, Kimiko joined her, rolling down the window to catch the breeze. The air was crisp; the sun was warm. It all felt perfect.

When they arrived, the convention was already packed with fans, a lot of them wearing elaborate, wild cosplay costumes.

"That's so rad," Allie whispered about a guy with bright yellow foam rubber hair that stood about two feet off his head, streaming out in all directions.

They meandered through the live action role-play area, took turns at a Sailor Moon video game, and listened to a panel about boys' love. All the while, Kimiko giggled along with Allie. It seemed like ever since they'd first met, they were both giggling constantly.

"Hey, Allie!" a group of girls called as they were leaving the boys' love session.

"Hi, guys," Allie waved and turned to Kimiko. "These are my friends from our manga club."

"'Sup?" Kimiko said, feeling suddenly out of place as Allie talked and joked with the group. Even though they seemed nice, they were all WASPy girlie girls.

"Would you rather hang out with them?" Kimiko whispered to Allie as the group left. "If you do, I understand."

"No. I see them all the time. I'd rather hang out with you."

"Really?" Kimiko replied with a smile. "Cool."

They next watched an anime film, managing to get the last two seats together in the warm, packed room. The minty scent of Allie's lip gloss wafted across the darkness, and Kimiko breathed it in.

After the movie, they wandered to the merchandise area and flipped through mangas. Allie picked up copies of *Tokyo Mew Mew* and *Instant Teen: Just Add Nuts.* When they got to the girls' love section, she asked, "Which do you like?"

"*Revo Girl Utena* is good," Kimiko said, "but wicked surreal. *Read or Dream* is also good, though my fave is *Girl Panic.*" She handed Allie the first installment and watched her expression as she scanned the pages.

"It looks fun," Allie said, nodding approval.

"I'll get it for you," Kimiko offered.

"All right." Allie giggled. "But then I get to treat for eats."

They paid for their mangas, got some frozen yogurt, and sat down on a patch of carpet at the edge of the crowded convention hallway.

"I'm so happy you came," Allie said. "This is such a blast. Chip isn't into manga."

Chip? Kimiko wondered. *Oh, yeah. The Boyfriend.*

"He's a wonderful guy," Allie continued. "I like him a lot, but . . ." She chewed on her lip for a moment, debating if she should confide her recent doubts. "I'm not sure where our relationship is going. I don't feel the same connection anymore. You know what I mean?"

"Are you breaking up?" Kimiko asked, a little surprised. She felt flattered that Allie was opening up to her so much, considering they barely knew each other.

"It's not to the point of breaking up yet. But I wonder if that's where it's headed." She was glad she'd decided to talk about it to Kimiko—somebody who was impartial and didn't go to her school.

"Have you talked with him about it?" Kimiko asked.

"Not yet. I'm still trying to figure out what to say. I don't want to hurt him. . . ." She gave Kimiko a questioning glance. "Any ideas?"

Me? Kimiko thought. "Sorry, dude. I have like zero experience with relationships. I guess just be honest with him."

"Yeah, that's what Lance says."

They sat quietly, eating their yogurt, watching the crowd. And a question that Allie had been curious about drifted into her mind.

"Can I ask you something? How did you realize that you liked girls? I mean—you know—as more than just friends?"

Kimiko stared at her, caught off guard, and recalled Sergio's teasing about Allie being "bi-curious."

"Well . . ." Kimiko stirred her spoon in her yogurt, deciding where to start. "I always felt different from other girls. At first I thought it was because I'm Asian, but then . . . I remember this party in like sixth grade when we played Eleven in Heaven? You know that game where some random boy and girl go into a closet for eleven seconds, supposedly to kiss, while the people outside count down?"

Allie nodded, remembering her own experiences with middle school parties.

"Well, when I got inside," Kimiko continued, "I realized there was no way I wanted to kiss a boy. So I told him that I had mono. Of course I didn't, really. And I buried my face in the clothes rack, although I felt kind of bad for him."

The story was so different from Allie's experience: She'd wanted to kiss boys since she could remember and, despite her doubts about Chip, she still thought guys were hot.

"After that," Kimiko continued, "one day I saw these two women on a motorcycle. Actually, I wrote a poem about it. Poetry is like my über-passion. . . ." She thought carefully for a moment about the impulse she was feeling. "Would you like to hear it?" It amazed her that she'd asked, considering she hardly knew Allie.

"Like, *yeah*!" Allie replied excitedly. "I love poems."

"Really? Okay . . ." Kimiko chewed nervously on her yogurt spoon, hoping she'd be able to remember the lines without screwing up. "It's called 'To the Two Women on a Harley at the Intersection of Twelfth and Independence.'"

"I like the title," Allie said, smiling with encouragement.

Kimiko took a breath, collecting her thoughts, and began:

"It's the morning of my twelfth birthday and
Mom has taken me shopping downtown.
While waiting to cross the street, we notice
two women stopped on a motorcycle,
engine throttling. The woman seated in front turns
and kisses the woman behind her.
On the lips.

I'm aware of my mom beside me, shifting her feet from one to the other,

clutching my hand.

Our eyes are glued to the women and I hear an 'Ah!' of understanding.

It's my mom's voice, soft and low—except it escapes from my mouth, from *me*.

Mom and I, we're spinning off the curb, realizing: You, Kimiko, you're one of *them*.

I try to stop the feeling of floating into the hot blue sky.

How has this happened? What has made me one of them?

I glance down at my boy's jeans and flannel shirt.

The sun slips behind a cloud and appears again.

The traffic light changes, the Harley roars away.

Nothing so weird has ever happened to me, and nothing more weird could ever happen.

Mom lets go of my hand and tells me,

'Be careful, promise?'"

Kimiko let out a breath, relieved that she'd actually made it through the poem without messing up. She stared at Allie, waiting for her reaction.

"Wow," Allie said softly. "You write beautifully."

"Thanks," Kimiko said, proud but turning red. "So

anyway . . . You asked me how I knew I liked girls. I think seeing those two women helped me figure out that's what I wanted: to one day be in love with a girl." She grinned awkwardly. "And have a motorcycle."

Allie thought about Jenny's boyfriend, Jack, who had a motorbike. Then she thought about something else: "I had a sex dream about a girl once."

Kimiko stared at her, even more astounded than before. "You did?"

"Only once," Allie clarified, suddenly nervous. "Anyway, I wanted to ask you: Do you think some people are truly bi? Lance doesn't. He thinks bi is kind of a cop-out. He says people are born either gay or straight. What do you think?"

"Well . . ." Kimiko paused and watched the crowd passing by. "Did you ever hear of this famous doctor-dude named Kinsey? He did research on like hundreds of people back in the fifties. And he found that some people are super-straight, some are über-homo, and most people are actually somewhere in between."

Allie shifted on the carpet. "So does that dream mean *I'm* in between?"

"I don't know. . . ." Kimiko tugged at the collar of her borrowed cowboy shirt, feeling warm, in spite of the frozen yogurt. "Maybe you should talk to Sergio. He's the bi expert, not me."

Allie glanced down at the *Girl Panic* manga that Kimiko had bought her. She was glad that they'd talked about this stuff, but it felt like they'd gone far enough for now.

"So, what's your favorite anime?" she asked, switching topics.

They talked for a while longer about anime characters and plots, Miyazaki movies, the GSA club at school, and other stuff, until Allie realized she needed to go.

"It's date night," she said, pulling her compact out. "You're so lucky you can get away without wearing makeup. I'd look like a pancake."

"Dude, I doubt that." Kimiko couldn't imagine Allie looking anything like a pancake.

On the ride back to Kimiko's, they sang along to some Mamas and the Papas songs.

"I had a really great time today," Kimiko said when they got to her house.

"Me too," Allie said, smiling across the car as if she didn't want to leave. "Let's talk again soon, okay? Oh, here!" She grabbed the daisy from the little dashboard vase and held it out to Kimiko. "I'd like you to have it."

"Thanks," Kimiko said. She tried to make her heart slow down as she took the flower and opened the door.

And as she watched Allie drive away, she thought about what Sergio had said. Had that been a date? It had almost felt like one.

After dropping Kimiko off, Allie phoned Lance, knowing he'd probably be nervous before his date with Sergio. "Hey, babe. How's it going?"

"I'm a wreck," he said, pulling a shirt on. "I just found a gray hair. How can I be getting gray hair already?"

"Where was it?" Allie asked, holding back a giggle.

"On my head, where else?" He stepped into a pair of freshly laundered jeans. "Oh, yeah." He laughed. "No, it was on my head. So, how did it go with Kimiko?"

"Super! She gave me this girls' love manga and recited an amazing poem she wrote. Oh my god, you've got to hear it! And I told her about that girl dream I had once. Remember that?"

"Yeah." Lance stepped into a pair of loafers without socks. "How did *that* come up?"

"Well, I remembered it the other day, and it was really easy talking with her, and I wanted to get her take on it. She told me about this doctor named Kinsey who said that most people are somewhere in between gay and straight. . . ."

While Lance listened, his mind wandered to Sergio. He knew he needed to talk more with him about the bi thing. He tugged at his belt, uneasy at the prospect.

". . . And I told her about Chip," Allie continued. "Like you, she told me I should be honest with him. But I'm still trying to figure out how I feel and what to say. Maybe I should suggest we take a break while I figure things out. What do you think?"

"That sounds good, I guess." Lance checked himself in the mirror one last time. "I wish I could be more help on what to say but I don't know."

"That's all right," Allie said. "I'll be okay. Have fun with Sergio! I want a full report."

"Thanks, and you with Chip," Lance told her. After hanging up, he raced downstairs, where he yelled to his parents: "I'm going to wait outside!"

"I want to meet him before you leave," his mom called after Lance. She seemed nearly as excited about his date as he was.

He let his dog out with him and sat down on the front steps, humming to himself, too anxious to wait inside.

Sergio was only a few streets away from Lance's when Kimiko phoned him.

"Go ahead, caller," Sergio answered. "You're on the air. How was your date with Allie?"

"I had a great time," Kimiko said, closing her bedroom door so her parents wouldn't hear. "But it felt a little weird. She told me she'd had a sex dream about a girl."

"Yee-hah!" Sergio tooted the car horn in excitement.

"Shush, dude," Kimiko said. "She said it only happened once. But maybe you're right: She is bi-curious—or at least questioning. I told her she should talk with you."

"Sure, I'd be happy to," Sergio said, adding, "I'd better talk to Lance about it too. Hey, I'm almost at his house—just turned onto his street."

"Are you nervous?" Kimiko asked.

"Not really. Well, some, I guess . . . There he is! I'll give you the postmortem later."

He hung up and parked as Lance strode down the front walkway of the big colonial-style two-story—all six-foot-plus of him, his jeans crispy clean and his hair freshly trimmed. At his side, an Irish setter bounded, barked, and wagged its tail. Sergio checked himself in the visor mirror and climbed out of the car while Lance grabbed the dog's collar and patted him to calm down.

"Hi, meet Rufus. He gets excited easily."

"No prob." Sergio stroked the dog's fur as it nuzzled into him. "So long as he doesn't pee on me. Hey, I like your haircut."

"Thanks. Come inside. Mom and Dad want to meet you."

"Really? What did you tell them?"

"That we're going on a date." Lance grinned, his sticky-outy ears turning red.

"Wows!" Sergio exclaimed. "You were serious about being out to them."

Mrs. Newsome was practically waiting by the door when Lance led Sergio inside. "You must be the Sergio we've been hearing about."

"Mom!" Lance protested, blushing again.

In the family room, Mr. Newsome stood up from reading *The New Yorker* and shook hands. "It's nice to meet you."

Rufus brought a squeaky toy and pawed at Sergio to play fetch while Lance's dad and mom asked parenty questions about school and home. It amazed Sergio how at ease they were that their son had a date with a guy. He wished his folks were that relaxed. Mrs. Newsome had the same blond hair and freckles as Lance. Mr. Newsome seemed so gentle and soft-spoken, to the point of almost . . .

"So, um, is your dad gay?" Sergio kidded Lance when they went out to the car.

"Nyeah." Lance laughed. "Although sometimes I think he sounds even gayer than me. Yeah, I love my gay straight dad."

When they climbed inside the car, Lance's cologne wafted toward Sergio.

"You wear FIERCE, don't you?"

"Uh-oh. Did I put too much on?"

"No," Sergio said, starting the ignition. "It's one of my favorites."

During the drive to the mall, they listened to the stereo and asked each other fluffy questions like: "So, um, boxers or briefs?"

"I'm a boxers guy," Lance volunteered. "How about you?"

"Commando!" Sergio said. "Ready for action."

Lance blushed at the thought of Sergio without underwear. This was their first time alone together, and the energy between them felt almost strong enough to power the car.

"If you could meet anybody in the world," Lance asked, "who would you choose?"

"Paris Hilton!" Sergio answered and watched Lance cringe. "Okay, I know she's a mess," Sergio added, "but she's so willing to be who she is—one hundred percent."

"True, I'll give you that."

"Your turn," Sergio said and Lance told him: "Johnny Depp. I think he's the best actor ever."

"Man, I'm so with you!" Sergio high-fived him. "I'd give any body part to meet him—well, almost any."

For dinner, they returned to the mall food court where they'd first met. Lance got a couple of cheeseburgers and some fries from the burger joint, while Sergio ordered a chicken bruschetta dripping with pesto sauce from an Italian place.

"You want to taste?" Sergio held the sandwich out.

"Mmm, that's delish," Lance said, taking a bite. He liked how Sergio coaxed him to try new things, getting him out of his comfort zone.

They talked about favorite ethnic foods. Lance liked Chinese. Sergio liked everything: Thai, Lebanese, Indian. . . . They discussed sports: Lance was on the swim team; Sergio liked to work out. And they talked about growing up.

"So, like when did you first figure out you liked guys?" Lance asked.

"I knew since I was little," Sergio said and grabbed the chance to get back to the bi issue. "Just as I knew I liked *girls*. I liked *both*. It seemed so natural. I thought everyone was bi."

Lance chewed on his burger, trying to figure out how to respond without being confrontational.

"But if you're attracted to guys," he told Sergio, "doesn't that make you gay? I mean straight guys aren't attracted to other guys—right?"

"Yeah," Sergio agreed. "But neither are gay guys attracted to girls—right? I mean are you?"

"No." The mere idea of girl-sex made Lance feel a little woozy. Not that he had anything against heterosexuals; he just never wanted to be one. He loved being gay.

"That's the difference," Sergio said, "between being gay and being bi. I *am* attracted to girls."

"But let's say," Lance persisted, "that you saw a smokin' hot guy and a sizzling cute girl both at the same time. Which one would you choose?"

Sergio thought for a moment. "I'd want to sandwich myself in between them. *He he he.*"

Lance laughed too—a little nervously. Could Sergio seriously be bi? Or was he just being hypothetical? He forced himself to ask: "So, um . . . have you ever actually . . . gotten sexual with a girl?"

Sergio braced himself. "Yep."

"Really?" Lance winced at the thought of Sergio

actually doing it with a female person. He put his burger down, unable to eat anymore, while Sergio told him about his girl experiences, culminating with his falling in love with Zelda and losing his "hetero-ginity."

He's already had full-on sex, Lance thought, *with a GIRL! ON PURPOSE!*

Besides making him queasy, it made him feel like an immature kid. The most he'd ever done with Darrell was an oral sex attempt that had kind of crashed and burned.

As Sergio told Lance about his breakup with Zelda, his voice became soft and raspy; his eyes turned wet and shiny. And he noticed Lance squirming. But at least the dude listened. That was a cut above most guys. Lance's attention encouraged him to open up even more, confessing about his past hookups. *May as well come clean about everything up front*, he figured.

Lance leaned back in his seat, feeling even more naive and inexperienced—and worried. With how *many* guys had Sergio hooked up? Did he expect sex *tonight*? Lance wasn't ready to go that far, especially on their first date. How would he get out of it? He wished he'd driven his own car.

And yet at the same time, he respected Sergio for being so open and one hundred percent honest about himself. No wonder he admired Paris Hilton.

"So, um . . ." Lance ventured nervously. "What about now? Are you over Zelda? And, um, over doing hookups?"

"Yeah. I'd like to at least try a relationship with a guy . . . see if it can work. I mean, sex with guys is easy, but sometimes I wonder about a relationship. You know, because of all the male ego caca, the arguments about who's right, each wanting to be top dog, all that alpha male crappage? It's simpler with girls. They've got less ego, less need to be right. They're easier to get along with. Don't you find that with Allie?"

"Yeah," Lance agreed. Sometimes he'd wondered why he couldn't find a guy he got along with as well as he did with Allie. "But I think it can work with a guy. I've seen guy couples on TV who have been together a long time. They made it work."

"Have you been in a relationship with a guy?" Sergio asked.

"Um, yeah, sort of." He wanted to be as honest as Sergio had been, while at the same time worrying: Would Sergio dump him once he'd revealed what a sex and relationship nerd he was? And what if Sergio didn't ditch him? Did Lance want to get involved with a guy who had a history of sleeping around, including with girls?

Lance took a deep breath, and then several more, as he told Sergio about his pitiful so-called love life.

"I hear you." Sergio nodded sympathetically. Listening to Lance's struggles made Sergio want to reach over and hold him, comfort him, encourage him. But it also worried him that—by the sound of it—Lance was still a virgin. On one hand, he liked the possibility of showing and teaching Lance stuff. . . . But what if things didn't work out between them? He didn't want to end up hurting him. The dude seemed so wholesome, innocent, vulnerable.

"It's frustrating," Lance continued, "to see Darrell together with a girl—not that I'm jealous; I'm really not. I just feel like he should tell her the truth."

"What do you mean?" Sergio asked. "What truth?"

"You know, that he's gay."

"Well, maybe he's bi," Sergio said, growing a little uneasy. The tone of the conversation was clearly changing: turning tense.

"He's not bi," Lance replied, crossing his arms. "He's a closet case. He's lying."

Sergio leaned back in his seat, a scowl pulling at his lips. "How can you say for sure he's not bi?"

"Because . . ." Lance hesitated, preparing for what he'd held back from discussing. "I don't believe there really is such a thing as being bi."

"What do you mean you don't 'believe' it?" Sergio asked, trying to keep cool. "Do you mean that in the same way that homophobes don't believe gay people are really gay? Are you like bi-phobic?"

"No!" Lance had never foreseen being compared with a homophobe. "I just think that you're born either gay or straight. One or the other."

"Just because you were," Sergio replied, "that doesn't mean everybody is. Don't you think it's a little bit arrogant for you to judge other people's sexual orientation?"

Lance felt his temper suddenly spike. He didn't appreciate being told he was arrogant. "I'm not judging people."

"Yeah, you are. You think that bi people are lying. What about me? Do you think I'm lying?"

"No," Lance faltered. "But just because you had sex with a girl—or girls—I don't think that makes you bi."

"Then what's it make me?" Sergio asked. "A closet case? But I'm not in the closet. I'm out as bi. Why can't you accept that some people like both guys and girls? Just because you don't understand it, does that mean other people can't feel that way? Why is it such an issue for you anyway?"

Lance's thoughts were swimming. This conversation was going even worse than he'd ever imagined.

"Fine! You win. You're bi. So if you think it's easier to be with a girl, then why did you ask me out?"

"Because . . ." Sergio softened his tone. "Like I said, man, I want to see if it can work with a guy . . . and because . . ." He gave a lopsided smile. " . . . I like you."

Hearing that, Lance calmed down a little. He'd never expected Sergio to tell him he *liked* him on a first date.

"Look," Sergio continued. "I'm sorry if I hurt your feelings. I just get tired of people not accepting me for who I am."

It impressed Lance to hear him apologize so readily. Maybe he should apologize also. "I'm sorry too. I didn't mean to judge you. I just don't understand how somebody can switch between guys and girls."

"It's not 'switching,'" Sergio said. "It's just accepting different sides of myself."

Lance thought about that. "Well, maybe you're right: A relationship with a girl would be easier. But that's not an option for me. Maybe that's why I don't want to believe in bi people. It feels sort of unfair that you have that choice and I don't."

"Wow," Sergio said. He liked how Lance had been able to turn his views around so quickly. He might be inexperienced, but he wasn't immature. "I never thought of it that way."

"Neither had I," Lance admitted. Their date so far hadn't played out like the Broadway musical he'd hoped it would. And yet it felt like he was connecting with Sergio in a way he never had with Darrell or any other boy.

"So, do you still want to see a movie?" Lance asked as they left the food court.

"Yeah," Sergio said. "Do you?"

"Yeah," Lance replied.

At the multiplex, they settled on a buddy bromance that looked funny from the poster. Sergio bought their tickets, feeling a little guilty that he might have been too hard on Lance. But he still wondered: Could a relationship with him work? Maybe they should just be friends.

Halfway through the film, Lance slowly took hold of his hand. *So much for just being friends*, Sergio thought.

It felt good to hold Lance's hand. Among his hook-ups, Sergio couldn't remember ever just holding hands with a guy. This was new, different. It reminded him of Zelda before things nosedived.

"How did you like it?" Sergio asked when the final credits rolled on-screen.

"Um, I liked it," Lance said, though in truth he'd

barely paid attention. Holding Sergio's hand had distracted him too much. "How about you?"

"It was great," Sergio said, stalling for time as the lights came on. Holding hands had produced a noteworthy effect that kind of embarrassed him to stand up. Being only friends definitely wasn't going to work.

"What would you like to do now?" Sergio asked when they finally walked outside to the parking lot. Part of him hoped for a little action—maybe they could go park somewhere—while another part of him could hear Kimiko telling him: "Go slow."

"I should probably head home," Lance said, glancing at his watch. "I've got church tomorrow. I'm in the choir with Allie."

"Oh," Sergio said, let down but also relieved.

On the walk to the car, Lance began to hum some show tune. "Um, sorry." He realized he was doing it. "I've always got musicals going through my head."

"That's cool," Sergio said. "I like your voice." He kept the stereo off during the drive so he could hear him sing. He'd never had a guy sing for him before. And Lance had never gone out with a guy who wanted him to sing.

When they arrived in front of Lance's, Sergio shut the engine off, wondering and hoping: Would Lance at least want to kiss?

Across the car, Lance became quiet, noticing how sexy Sergio's Adam's apple looked in the moonlight. Since they'd held hands, it seemed natural that they would kiss, but he felt a little nervous about his lack of experience. Darrell had never really been into kissing, and Allie's pecks didn't count.

He quickly glanced out the window to check if anyone was watching. Nope; they were alone, just the two of them. His pulse quickened as he returned his gaze to Sergio. "Um, do you like to kiss?"

"Yeah." Sergio loved to kiss. He'd missed it since he'd broken up with Zelda.

He unbuckled his shoulder strap, while Lance fumbled with his own. And then they were leaning into each other. Sergio tilted his head a little, his breath warming Lance's cheek, and Lance closed his eyes, accidentally bumping Sergio's nose. Then their mouths gently landed on each other's, and their lips connected. Sergio's tongue slipped easily into Lance's mouth, tapping his tongue, tasting fresh and clean. And Lance tapped him back—his first time ever to French-kiss.

"You kiss great," Sergio whispered, when at last they pulled away.

"Thanks." Lance opened his eyes, smiling proudly. "You're a great kisser too."

"Thanks," Sergio echoed.

Lance drew toward him, wanting more, and once again accidentally bumped Sergio's nose. "Um, sorry."

"I know it's big," Sergio said. "When I have enough money, I want to get it done."

"No," Lance replied. "I like it."

"Really?" Nobody had ever told Sergio *that* before.

"Yeah," Lance assured him. "I'm the one who needs my ears flattened."

"Nah, man! I think they're cute."

"That's good," Lance said. Then they were kissing again, going at it more passionately than before. Sergio no longer worried about Lance being a virgin—he definitely didn't kiss like one.

His hands moved across Lance's chest, wanting to touch and feel and go as far as Lance would let him.

To Lance, it no longer troubled him that Sergio was bi or how many people he'd slept with. All that mattered was the thrill of running his fingers through Sergio's hair, breathing in the scent of his skin, losing himself in Sergio's jaw line. . . .

But as the blood pulsed through his arteries, things started to feel too intense, too fast. He wanted to get to know Sergio more first; he wanted this to be special; he wanted them to take their time. He needed to stop.

"I had a great time," he told Sergio, forcing himself to pull away.

"Me too," Sergio said, catching his breath while wishing they could keep going. "You really do kiss great."

"Well, you're the first guy I, um, ever kissed like that," Lance admitted. "With tongue and everything. The first person ever. Darrell was never very into kissing."

"Oh, yeah?" Sergio said, his doubts returning: Lance was even more of a virgin than he'd imagined. "Wow."

"So, um, good night, I guess," Lance said, reluctantly reaching for the door handle.

"Good night," Sergio murmured sadly, not wanting their time to end.

He watched Lance cross the yard, kind of hoping he'd turn around and come back. At the top of the front steps, Lance turned and waved good-bye. Sergio waved back, waiting until Lance went inside before he drove away.

After saying good night to his parents, Lance hurried upstairs, excited to phone Allie about his date with Sergio—and eager to find out about her evening with Chip.

CHAPTER SIX

"Whoa, these girls are kissing!" Chip had exclaimed earlier that evening when he climbed into Allie's VW and noticed the *Girl Panic* manga.

"It's a girls' love manga," Allie explained as she drove them to dinner.

"I didn't know they made stuff like this." He flipped through the pages, looking for more make-out pictures. It was the first time he'd paid any attention to her manga. "Where did you get it?"

"At the convention, from Kimiko. Remember the Japanese-American girl who wrote my name in kanji?"

"Oh, yeah." Not finding any more exciting drawings, he put the manga aside. "So, is she bi?"

"No." Allie recalled her conversation with Kimiko. "She's only into girls."

"Oh," Chip said, in a tone Allie couldn't identify.

"Why?" she asked.

"Just wondering."

While she told him about the anime convention, he reached over and stroked her hair.

"Where's the flower you usually have?" he asked, noticing the empty dashboard vase.

"I gave it to her," Allie said. Then, on impulse, she asked him, "Have you ever had a sex dream about a guy?"

"Huh?" His forehead furrowed and his tone became strained. "No! Where did *that* question come from?"

"Just curious," she said. After continuing along the road for several minutes, she asked, "Have you ever wondered what it might be like to make out with a guy?"

"No!" Chip reiterated even more testily. "What's up with these questions?"

Allie bit into her bottom lip for a moment before answering. "One time I had a sex dream about a girl."

"You did?" His eyes widened a little and his voice relaxed. "Wow. When? Like what did you do in it?"

"We kissed," she said. "It was a long time ago, in middle school." The memory of it still made her skin tingle. "And we—you know—touched each other. . . . I mostly just remember how intense it was."

"I bet!" Chip nodded eagerly.

His enthusiasm surprised and confused her. Why was he so intrigued by her dream but so horror-struck at the thought of having sex with another guy?

"I never told anybody at school about the dream except Lance," she explained. "So don't mention it to anyone, okay?"

"Sure," Chip said, still imagining her and another girl kissing.

At the local diner, they met up with their friends

Jenny and Jack. They'd become a couple two months ago and ever since Jenny had stuck to Jack like Velcro, calling him her "better three-quarters."

Now, as they ate dinner and talked, Allie tried to remember: Had she ever felt that moony over Chip? She loved him in the sense that she cared about him, but she didn't feel the gushiness that Jenny did with Jack, at least not anymore. Why didn't she? What had changed?

After dinner they went to watch an action flick that the guys wanted to see. Jenny cuddled up beside Jack, kissing him at the end of practically every other scene. Meanwhile, Allie's mind wandered back to the anime convention . . . to Kimiko's poem about the two women . . . and to Lance— she hoped he was having a good time with Sergio. . . .

When the movie was over, the couples said good night and Allie watched Jenny ride away on the back of Jack's motorcycle. Then she and Chip returned to his bungalow and took their usual places in front of the TV.

She knew she needed to say something before they settled into making out—but she still wasn't sure what to say. Although both Lance and Kimiko had urged her to be honest, it would feel cruel to tell Chip she didn't feel in love with him anymore. She nervously twirled a curl of hair between her fingertips.

"I think maybe we should take a break," she announced.

Chip blinked, obviously caught by surprise. "A break from what?"

"From . . ." Allie's voice quavered, " . . . from spending so much time together."

He blinked again, studying her. "I thought you liked to spend time together."

"I do," she said, resting her hand on his arm. "I just think maybe it would be good for us to take a break."

"What did I do wrong?" he asked.

"You didn't do anything wrong. It's about me, not you."

"Okay, then—so what's going on with you?" His brow wrinkled up as he struggled to understand. "It feels like you're not telling me something. Does it have to do with that girl dream?"

"Maybe." She shifted her feet on the carpet. "I don't know. I just feel like I need to sort some things out. Stuff I mentioned before . . . about our future?"

He glanced away and thought for a moment, then looked back at her. "For how long do you want to take a break?"

"I'm not sure," she said honestly.

"All right," he said, leaning back. "Then I guess I'll wait."

His response didn't exactly make sense to Allie. "Wait? For what?"

"I'll wait for you," he replied, taking hold of her hand, " . . . for as long as it takes."

She hadn't foreseen that. She'd figured he might feel hurt or pouty but not this.

"I love you," he said, leaning forward to kiss her.

"I love you too," she answered, although she felt more confusion than love.

When she got into her car to drive home, she checked

her cell for missed calls hoping to find one from Lance. But there weren't any and she didn't want to interrupt his date with Sergio.

Once she got home to her room, she tried to take her mind off Chip by diving into the *Girl Panic* manga from Kimiko.

The story took place at an all-girls' high school and opened with Katsuko, a tomboy, falling in love with Ayumi, a girlie girl whose beauty "stole Katsuko's breath away."

Ayumi reciprocated the crushy feelings, leading to much angst, wacky chaos, and dialog that cracked Allie up—like when Ayumi said, "If you really love me, buy me doughnuts."

And Katsuko replied, "Okay, but don't blame me if you get fat."

At the climax, a jealous classmate convinced the girls that they'd each betrayed the other. But in the end, Katsuko and Ayumi reconciled with the full-on lip-lock that had grabbed Chip's attention. And when Allie closed the last page, she felt a warm glow inside. No wonder the story was Kimiko's favorite.

Noticing that it was almost midnight, Allie decided to go to bed and catch up with Lance in the morning. But first she sent Kimiko a text that said, *Thanx, loved Girl Panic. But don't blame me if I get fat.* ☺

When she'd gotten home from the manga convention that afternoon, Kimiko had pressed the daisy Allie had given her into her poetry notebook.

After dinner, her creative writing classmate, Serena,

had come over so they could read their latest poems and give each other feedback. When Serena returned home, Kimiko felt inspired by her encouragement to keep working on her poem. For the rest of the evening, she typed and retyped words, shifted stanzas, moved sentences . . . .

One minute she loved what she'd written. The next moment she hated it. Writing was always like that for her. The words never lived up to the feelings she wanted to express. From the very first word she put on paper, it seemed as though the poem was already ruined.

Tonight was no different. Her eyes were blurry from fatigue as she read over what she'd written:

THE WORLD'S SIX TRILLIONTH LOVE POEM
    POEMS ABOUT LOVE AREN'T REALLY;
    THEY'RE ABOUT WANTING THE WRONG
PERSON, THE ONE WHO
    DOESN'T LOVE YOU BACK. THEY'RE ABOUT
    LUST, JEALOUSY, ENVY, LOSS. ABOUT
    FALSE PROMISES, SHATTERED DREAMS,
BROKEN HEARTS. ABOUT
    TEARS, LAUGHTER, REJECTION, DEATH,
EVERYTHING EXCEPT
    LOVE.
    POEM UPON POEM, SONNET
    AFTER SONNET. ALL WITH THE SAME
REFRAIN:
    "HAVE HOPE! YOU MUST! KEEP LOVE
ALIVE!"
    SO WE KEEP READING THEM, WRITING

THEM, AND THINKING:
   MAYBE THIS ONE
   WILL BE DIFFERENT.

Kimiko let out a breath, still dissatisfied. Despite Serena's encouragement, she still wasn't happy with it. But she didn't know what else to change. She knew from experience that she could work on it till dawn and she still wouldn't be content. Might as well just give up and hit DELETE.

"That means it's time to put it aside," Ms. Swann, her creative writing teacher always told the class.

Exhausted, Kimiko hit SAVE and closed the file. She was changing into her pajamas when her cell rang.

"He's a virgin," Sergio announced as soon as she answered. "He's never even French-kissed—until tonight."

"Wow," Kimiko said, taking off her cap and sliding into bed. "He must really like you."

"Huh?" Sergio asked, stopping at a traffic light.

"If you're the first person he's ever Frenched," Kimiko explained, "he must think you're really special."

"Well, that's pressure!" Sergio said, gripping the steering wheel more tightly. "What if I don't live up to what he's expecting?"

"Well, you can't control what he expects. All you can do is be yourself."

"Yes, Oprah," Sergio said, continuing down the road. "At least we hashed out the bi thing. I think he finally got it. I feel like his teacher, which I kind of like. And I told him about Zelda and about hooking up. Man, I was a blabbermouth."

"It's good you put it all out there."

"Yeah. I'm amazed he didn't freak out."

"That's a good sign."

"It's hard to believe he's a virgin. Damn, he's a great kisser. Frickin' gifted! How is it nobody's snatched him up?"

"So does that mean there will be a second date?" Kimiko asked, just as her cell phone beeped. "Hold on! I got a text."

"Let me guess," Sergio said as she came back on. "Is it from your date this afternoon?"

"Shush, dude!"

"So what does she say?"

"That she liked the *Girl Panic* manga I gave her."

Sergio burst into a laugh. "You gave her a girl-girl love story?"

"Well, she'd never read one before. I was just being friendly."

"And she liked it, huh? She is *so* bi."

"She's just being polite. Let me text her back." She wrote to Allie: *Glad u liked it. Hope 2 c u again soon!*

She continued to talk with Sergio until he arrived home. When he got to his room, he went online to check messages and found an IM from Lance: *Thanx 4 a great time.*

Should I reply? Sergio wondered; although he'd enjoyed the time with Lance, this was starting to feel a little too gooey.

Ditto, he wrote back. Then he undressed and climbed between the sheets, eager to relive their make-out session—and more.

CHAPTER SEVEN

"So, tell me what I missed," Allie said when Lance picked her up for church choir the next morning. "What happened with Sergio? Where did you go? What did you do? I want the full lowdown."

A sheepish little smile tugged at Lance's lips. "We made out."

"Woo-hoo!" Allie high-fived him. "And how was it?"

"Sweet! He said I'm a great kisser."

"See?" She squeezed his shoulder as he pulled out of the driveway. "I knew you two would be good together."

Lance pursed his lips, not quite as convinced. In the light of day, his doubts about Sergio had resumed.

"Uh-oh," Allie said. "Something's wrong, isn't it? This is face-viewing range. I can see it."

Lance let out a sigh, unsure he wanted to get into it before church. "Apparently, he truly is bi."

"I thought you didn't believe in bi people," Allie said.

"Now I do. He's already had full-on sex with both guys *and* girls." To make sure she got the point, he repeated: "And *girls!*"

"Babe?" Allie patted his hand. "Could you please not make it sound so awful?"

"Oops, sorry. I just don't get how somebody can get turned on by both. Being attracted to *one* seems complicated enough."

"I know!" Allie nodded in agreement, recalling her date the previous evening with Chip.

"It's like there's this straight part of him," Lance continued, "that I'll never be able to connect with—and I don't *want* to connect with it. Plus, he's also done hookups. Compared to him, I feel like I'm in the remedial dating group."

"But he thinks you're a great kisser," Allie said. "Give yourself some props."

"Yeah . . ." Lance smiled proudly, calming down as he remembered making out. "And he said he likes me—on our first date! That's more than I got from Darrell during the whole time we were together."

"Wow!" She raised her palm and high-fived him again. "And did you tell Sergio you like him?"

"No. It felt too soon. It's confusing; on one hand, it felt like we really connected, but on the other . . ." Lance stared out the windshield at the road ahead. "What if he ditches me for a girl?"

"Well, he could ditch you for a guy, too."

"Is that supposed to reassure me?"

"Or you might ditch him, too. Who can say what will happen?"

"Yeah." Lance tapped nervously on the steering wheel,

eager to talk about something else. "So, what happened with you and Chip? Did you talk to him about the stuff you told me?"

"Sort of. I told him I wanted to take a break. But then he kind of threw me for a loop. He said he'd wait for me for as long as it takes."

"He's going to *wait* for you?" Lance asked. "Wow! He really loves you, doesn't he?"

"Either that or he's a nut case."

"I wish I could find somebody like that," Lance said. "Not a nut case. I mean someone who—you know—we'd love each other that much."

"But the problem," Allie explained, "is that he loves me more than I love him. That's what makes this so hard. And you want to hear something weird? Before we talked, he got totally excited about the girls' love manga Kimiko gave me. And when I told him about that sex dream with the girl, I think he got turned on even more."

"What is it with straight guys and lesbians?" Lance laughed and turned the car into the church parking lot.

"I know, right? What a pair: He gets off on the thought of two girls together while I get off on the idea of two guys together."

And yet she'd also enjoyed the *Girl Panic* story. *So, what does that make me?* she wondered, still unsure. She felt relieved to get to choir so she could take her mind off of her identity drama—at least for a while.

* * *

That Sunday afternoon, Kimiko printed out her "World's Six Trillionth Love Poem" and took it to Sergio, her biggest, most devoted fan.

"Here. I worked on it last night." She unfolded the page from her jacket pocket and handed it to him. "I'm warning you—it's pretty crappy."

"I want you to read it to me," he said, refusing to take the poem.

She'd known he'd say that; he always did. But she didn't mind. It was good practice for poetry readings.

"Let me get comfy!" He hopped onto the bed, fluffed the pillows, and propped himself against the headboard. "Ready!"

Standing in front of him, she took a breath and read the poem. He listened closely, and when she'd finished, he leaped out of bed and chest-bumped her. "Bravo, man! I knew it would be great."

She shrugged, unflattered. "You'd think it was great even if I wrote about picking my nose."

"Because it would be!" He took the poem out of her hand and tacked it onto his wall. "So, what inspired you to write a love poem? Hmm . . . Could it have been your date with Allie?"

"I'm not listening," Kimiko said, plugging her fingers into her ears until he shushed. "I want to hear more about your date with Lance. So, when are you guys going out again?"

"I don't know. All morning long I've been thinking about him. . . ." While Sergio told her more about his time with Lance, he lifted his guinea pig, Elton, out of its cage and stroked its soft fur. ". . . A second date would be like the start of a relationship. You know what I mean? A first date is like a test drive; going out again would mean I want to buy the car."

"Not necessarily," Kimiko argued. "It just means you're willing to consider giving your love and affection to somebody who doesn't need wood shavings and eat food pellets."

"Ha-ha," Sergio said. "Besides, last time it was me who asked him out. This time it's his turn."

"Why are guys so competitive like that?" Kimiko asked.

"We're not competitive."

"Yes, you are."

"No, we're not."

"Yeah, you are."

"Okay, we are!" Sergio said and pretended to sic Elton on her.

During the following week, Sergio and Lance exchanged IMs several times—only about day-to-day stuff like classes or TV, nothing serious. While Sergio waited for Lance to ask him out, Serena, Kimiko's poetry classmate, kept chatting him up at lunch and between classes. She didn't really stoke his furnace like Zelda or Lance did, but she had a funny sense of humor, smelled good, and as Kimiko had put it, she did have "a nice rack."

"We should hang out sometime," Serena told him one day at his locker.

"Sure," he said, merely being friendly.

The next thing he knew she'd pulled out her cell. "What's your number?"

That very evening, she phoned him. And as with Zelda, he was upfront with her about being bi.

"Kimiko already told you that, right?"

"Yeah, that's cool," Serena said with a giggle. And even though it was only their first phone conversation, she asked, "You want to go out Saturday?"

He hadn't expected her to ask him out—at least not that quickly—and he wasn't sure if she meant it as a date or just as friends. But since he didn't have any plan for Saturday and Lance hadn't asked him out, he told her, "Okay."

They made a plan to see the new Tarantino movie, and as soon as he hung up he phoned Kimiko.

"Cool," Kimiko replied when he told her about the conversation. "Are you excited?"

"Not exactly. I'm not sure if this is a friend-date or a *date*-date."

"I guess you'll find out," Kimiko said with a giggle.

"I need the car this Saturday," Sergio told his mom and dad over dinner the following night.

"Oh?" his mom asked while serving him rice. "Who are you going out with?"

"Serena. She transferred from Northside. That's enough." He stopped his mom from serving him more. "I don't want to carb out."

"A new girl?" His dad's voice perked up. "That's good news."

"I'm not really interested in her," Sergio said, trying to temper his parents' enthusiasm. "It's more like a mercy date."

"You never know," his mom said, and he thought he saw her lips move in prayer.

When Saturday arrived, she gave him some home-made *churros* to take to Serena, and his dad slipped him a twenty for the date without Sergio even asking for it.

He shared the *churros* with Serena during their drive to the mall, while she talked about all sorts of stuff: how she'd learned to cook stir-fry, and how she missed a deaf friend at her old school, and about a jazz concert she'd gone to. She talked a lot more than Zelda or Lance—a whole lot more—and Sergio felt kind of relieved when the movie finally started.

About fifteen minutes into the film, she slipped her hand into his. But unlike with Lance, his pulse didn't ratchet up. He didn't particularly *mind* holding her hand; he just didn't feel *that way* about her. And during an action sequence, he casually pulled his hand away.

"Did you like it?" she asked after the movie had ended.

"I liked it all right," he said, standing up to stretch. "And you?"

"Yeah, me too." As they walked out of the theater, she discussed the different actors, and told him she was writing a screenplay, and explained how she thought screenplays were a lot like poetry.

When they stepped into the lobby, he glanced toward the candy counter. His heart nearly rocketed from his chest. Standing among the snack-buying crowd was Lance, looking as cute as Sergio remembered him—except for the fact he was with some guy.

Was the dude a date? Sergio wanted to say hi to Lance, but not if the guy was a date. That would be too awkward.

Just then, Lance turned in Sergio's direction. Upon spotting him, he broke into a huge smile.

"Let's say hi to my friend!" Sergio interrupted Serena and led her toward Lance. "What up, man?"

"Hi," Lance said, and his glance shifted to Serena, wondering: Was she a friend or a date? Had Sergio gone back to dating girls? Was that why he hadn't asked him out again? All week long he'd been hoping Sergio would call him, even while he hesitated to make the move himself.

"We just saw the new Tarantino flick," Sergio said. "What are you guys going to see?"

"The Proposal."

"Oh, yeah," Sergio said. "Chick flick, right?"

"Yeah," Lance said with a bashful grin. "Um . . ." He turned to the guy he was with. "This is my friend, Jamal."

"Hey," Jamal said. "How was the Tarantino?" It was the movie he'd wanted to see but Lance had talked him into *The Proposal.*

While Serena gave Jamal her rundown of the film, Sergio tried to get a clear vibe about him: Was he a friend-friend of Lance's or a date-friend? He never considered that Lance was wondering the same about Serena and him.

He wanted to pull Lance aside and ask: *Why haven't you called me, man?* But then Lance might ask the same of him. Instead, Sergio smiled awkwardly and Lance smiled awkwardly in return.

Serena finished her movie review and Sergio said, "Well, enjoy the show!"

"Thanks," Lance said and watched them leave. Where were they going? He wondered: to make out?

"Want some popcorn?" Jamal asked him.

"No, thanks," Lance mumbled, still watching Sergio.

Sergio peered over his shoulder, wanting to run back and tell Lance, "Hey, call me sometime!"

But not with Jamal there. Instead, he just waved and Lance waved back.

"Do you want to come over to my house for a while?" Serena asked when they got to Sergio's car.

"Huh?" His mind was still on Lance.

"My parents won't mind," Serena said. "They're cool." As Sergio drove toward her house, she told him how her parents had met during a high school football game and she was the oldest of three girls, and how the youngest had Down syndrome.

"Sorry to hear it," Sergio said, half-listening, all the while wishing he'd called Lance after their last date.

"Would you like to come in?" Serena asked when Sergio stopped in front of her house.

"Thanks, but . . ." Even though he'd enjoyed the time

with her, he just wasn't feeling any hots for her. ". . . Um, I think I'm ready to go home . . . if that's okay with you."

"No worries," Serena said. But she didn't move to open the door. Instead, she gazed across the seat at him, the quietest she'd been all evening.

He knew what she was waiting for. He wouldn't have minded kissing her except that it would imply something he didn't want to imply. On Monday he'd have to face her in school and he didn't want to give her the wrong idea.

"So . . . ," she said, making no endeavor to leave, even though he'd left the motor running. "Was that guy in the lobby somebody you went out with?"

"Huh?" Sergio turned to her. "Why do you ask that?"

"I got the vibe. He's cute. Nice smile. Tall! So, did you two go out?"

"Yeah," Sergio mumbled, a little embarrassed. "One time."

"I thought so." Serena grinned. "Do you have a crush on him?"

"A *crush*?" Sergio shuffled his feet on the floor mat. "No, why?"

"Because your whole face lit up when you saw him. I think he's got a crush on you, too."

"You do? What makes you say that?"

"He almost couldn't take his eyes off you—except when he was trying to figure out who I was."

"Oh, yeah?" It felt a little weird discussing all this since he hardly knew her. Plus, they were supposedly on a date. Or were they?

"So, was the Jamal guy a date or his boyfriend or something?" Serena asked.

"I'm not sure. I know he doesn't have a boyfriend."

"Then he's fair game for you." Serena gave him a puckish grin. "Call him!" She leaned across the seat, planted a kiss on Sergio's cheek, and opened the door to get out. "Thanks for a nice evening."

"Thanks to you, too," he replied, happy that she wasn't upset with how their evening had turned out. He waited until she got inside the house and waved goodbye. Then he drove away, his mind returning to Lance. Serena was right: He should call him—and find out his deal with Jamal.

"Guess what happened?" Lance told Allie over the phone as he headed home from dropping Jamal off. "I ran into Sergio at the movie theater."

"Oh, yeah?" Allie asked, in the middle of moisturizing before bed.

"Yeah, he was with a girl. *See?* This is the problem with dating someone bi. How am I supposed to know if she was a date or just a friend?"

"Well . . ." Allie rubbed the face cream into her cheeks. ". . . You could ask him."

"I'm not going to ask him that. I'm still not sure I want to get involved with him."

"Then why do you care if the girl was a friend or a date?"

Lance thought it over while stopped at a traffic light.

"All right, I'll call him." He let out a frustrated groan. "If he doesn't call me first. So, how was *your* evening?"

"My Saturday night felt a little weird without Chip," Allie replied. "I went bowling with Megan, Nancy, and Leo. That was fine. But I kept worrying about Chip, imagining him sitting home alone. I hope he's okay."

"He probably went out with his band buddies," Lance assured her as he turned onto his street. "Question is: Are *you* okay?"

"Yeah. A little sad, but okay. I'm still glad I suggested he and I take a break, to get perspective. You know?"

"Yep," Lance agreed and pulled into his driveway. "So, pick you up for church tomorrow?"

"Super," Allie said. "Good night, babe. Love you."

"Love you too," Lance whispered.

After hanging up, Allie climbed into bed and reached to turn the lamp off. Across the nightstand, Chip seemed to be staring straight at her from their photo. She turned the picture toward the wall and switched out the light.

Even though Allie and Chip had agreed to take a break, to carry it out at school was a little complicated, especially at lunch, since they both belonged to the same group. Chip still sat beside her, and at times he put his arm around her as though nothing had changed.

"What can I tell him?" Allie asked Lance one afternoon at their lockers. "I still feel guilty about him saying he'll wait for me."

"I guess he's showing you he means it," Lance said.

Hearing that didn't help her any. She wasn't sure what to tell other people, either. When Jenny heard they were taking a break from dating, she pulled Allie aside in the girls' room.

"What's going on with you and Chip? Why didn't

you tell me about it? Is something wrong?" Jenny lowered her voice to a whisper. "Are you seeing someone else?"

"No," Allie said. "I just need some time to think. That's all."

"Well," Jenny told her, "you know you can talk to me about anything."

"Thanks," Allie said, but for now she felt too confused to discuss it with her.

Meanwhile, she continued to chat online with Kimiko.

"I've thought about calling her," Kimiko told Sergio on the bus one day after school. "Maybe she'd want to hang out at the mall or something."

Kimiko expected Sergio to tease her about the idea but to her surprise, he didn't.

"Sure," he muttered, "call her. Why not?"

"You really think I should?" Kimiko asked. Even after the manga convention, she was still skeptical that an A-list girl like Allie would truly want to spend time with her.

"Just do it!" Sergio grumbled. He'd been edgy ever since running into Lance at the movie theater, especially since Lance still hadn't called him.

That evening, Kimiko closed her bedroom door, jiggled her arms and legs to shake out her nervousness, and dialed Allie's number.

"Hi!" Allie answered, putting aside her calculus homework. "I was going to call you."

"You were?" Kimiko asked, adjusting her cap.

"Yeah. Last night I reread *Girl Panic*. I really like it. Oh, and Chip was wowed by the drawing of the girls kissing. Why are straight boys so fascinated by the idea of two girls together?"

"Beats me." Kimiko pulled her cap off and scratched her head. "Maybe they think two is better than one? Like a harem?"

"Of course I'm no one to talk," Allie said, "considering that I think the idea of two *guys* making out is hot, hot, hot!"

Kimiko didn't understand that, either. She put her cap back on and told Allie, "To be honest, I don't really get why anybody would want to do anything with a guy. I remember the first time I saw a boy's thing. My mom was giving my little brother a bath, and I thought: *THAT wormy thing is what all the fuss is about?* I burst out laughing."

"Oh, I think guys' things are cute." Allie giggled. "It's funny how they pop up, like: Boing! There it goes!"

"Well . . ." Kimiko decided to change the subject. "If you liked *Girl Panic*, I can loan you Book Two. Sometimes sequels suck, but these are good."

"Yeah, I'd love that," Allie said.

"Okay, well . . ." Kimiko took a breath. "Do you want to, like, hang out sometime? I mean if you're not too busy—"

"How about Saturday?" Allie said. "In the afternoon? I've got a math competition in the morning."

"Math competition?"

"Yeah, I'm in Math Club. That's my nerdy side. I love

numbers like you love poetry. I'm always thinking about them. Like the other day waiting at the gas station? I looked around at the dollar amounts that people had paid and tried to guess who had been there. Like one pump said three-seventy and I figured that must've been a teenager with barely any money. Another pump said ten dollars and four cents and I knew they must have meant to do ten dollars but were a little slow, so maybe it was an old person. See what I mean?"

"Dude, I'm impressed," Kimiko said. She hadn't imagined that Allie had a nerdy side. Even though it made her less goddesslike, it also made her more human.

"I suck at math," Kimiko admitted. "It's like my *worst* subject. And my teachers expect me to be a genius with it 'cause I'm Asian. At the start of the year, they're so psyched to have me in their class. But by Thanksgiving they're like: 'Dude, are you *really* Japanese?'"

"Well," Allie said. "I'd be happy to help you."

"Really?" Kimiko didn't want to impose on her. "Thanks, I'll keep it in mind."

They talked a while longer and agreed to meet at the mall on Saturday. After hanging up, Kimiko shook her arms and legs out again—this time to release her joy.

On Saturday Kimiko put on the slinky red shirt Sergio had lent her—the one he'd worn on his date with Lance. The color matched her Harley baseball cap almost perfectly. Grabbing her leather jacket and the second *Girl Panic*, she headed downstairs to the backyard. Her dad was helping her mom spread some mulch on a flower bed.

"I'm going to the mall to meet Allie," Kimiko told them.

"Invite her back to visit," Kimiko's mom said. "I like her. She's very ladylike. Why don't you let your hair grow long like hers?"

Kimiko rolled her eyes. "Because I'm not her."

"Well, have a good time," her dad interjected, giving Kimiko the chance to leave before she and her mom got more on each other's nerves.

Kimiko arrived at the food court early and sat down by the fountain, then stood and searched the crowd, then sat down again, then stood up once more, too antsy to sit still. When Allie finally arrived, Kimiko greeted her excitedly with a fist-bump. "'Sup, dude?"

"Hi," Allie said. "I like your shirt."

"Thanks, it's share-wear from Sergio. So, how did your math competition go?"

"Awesome! Our team made second place."

"That's good. Here." She handed Allie Book Two of *Girl Panic*.

"Thanks!" Allie scanned the pages. "I can't wait to read it."

"So, do you want to hang out here?" Kimiko asked. "Or walk around?"

"Actually," Allie said. "I need to shop for some new bras. Would you mind?"

Kimiko gave a nervous giggle. Shop for lingerie with her? Seriously? She had to swallow the sudden knot in her throat before she could answer. "I don't, I-I mean: sure."

"Super!" Allie said. She often went shopping with friends, even for underthings. To her it was no big deal.

As they strolled out of the food court into the mall, Kimiko's brain felt frozen. She couldn't think of a single thing to say.

"I talked to Chip," Allie said, filling in the silence, "about him and me. You know, about the stuff I mentioned to you. Thanks for encouraging me to talk to him."

"No problem," Kimiko replied. "How did it turn out?"

Allie explained how she'd suggested they take a break.

"So you're not a couple anymore?" Kimiko asked.

"I'm not sure what we are," Allie answered, stopping at a women's store. "Let's try in here." As they walked to the lingerie section, she related to Kimiko how Chip had said he'd wait.

"Wait for *what?*" Kimiko replied.

"For me to make up my mind, I guess." Allie picked through a table of bras, trying to decide what she wanted. "I always have a hard time deciding. What kind do you like to wear?"

"Mostly sports bras," Kimiko said, blushing a little. She liked how they helped to flatten down her chest.

"Oh, really?" Allie asked. Then she lifted a pair of lacey bras. "Do you like these?"

"Um, for you, yeah." Kimiko tried to keep her face from flaming even more as she imagined Allie in one of the lacey bras.

"Let me go try them on," Allie said. "Come help me choose."

Kimiko waited outside the fitting room and took a few deep breaths to calm down. Was this really happening? Being invited along while trying on bras felt so like . . . *intimate*.

"Can you come look?" Allie cracked open the fitting booth curtain.

Kimiko thought it over for a nanosecond before moving over. "Um, sure. If you want."

"Does it look all right?" Allie asked, gazing at her bust in the mirror.

"It looks great." Kimiko practically choked the words out. "How does it feel?"

"Perfect." Allie ran her fingers beneath a strap and glanced at Kimiko. When their eyes met, an unexpected stirring moved through Allie. It was different from anything she'd ever experienced with any other girl, a sort of shyness coupled with desire.

"I really only need one." She giggled nervously, suddenly feeling exposed. "Should I get the black or the red one?"

"It's up to you, dude." Kimiko averted her eyes, trying not to stare.

"I'll get both," Allie said, too flustered to make a decision. "Thanks."

"No problem," Kimiko said, forcing herself to step back from the curtain.

It took a moment for Allie to regain her bearings. "Do

you need anything?" She asked as she carried the bras to the register.

"No, thanks," Kimiko said. "I'm good."

While they waited for the cashier, Allie returned to her conversation about Chip. "So anyway, I guess he's having a hard time letting go. He's really a nice guy. I think that's why this is so hard."

A stab of sadness pricked Kimiko. Even though she'd never met the guy, she felt sorry for him—and also sad for Allie having to go through this.

As Allie finished paying for the bras, she glanced up and her eyes widened. Her friend Jenny had just walked into the store, Jack trailing behind her. At the sight of her, an odd impulse overcame Allie. For some reason, she didn't want Jenny to see her with Kimiko.

"Let's go this way!" Allie whispered. She grabbed her shopping bag and circled toward the back of the store. Kimiko followed, glancing over her shoulder, trying to figure out what was going on.

"Allie!" Jenny called. "Allie!" But Allie kept walking down the aisle.

"Dude," Kimiko said, "that girl is calling you."

"Huh?" Allie stopped and feigned surprise as Jenny caught up to them in the jeans section.

"Hi! Didn't you hear me calling you?"

"No, I'm sorry," Allie lied. "How are you? I was just buying some stuff. So, yeah . . . What's up?"

"I'm dragging Jack around while I shop," Jenny said. She didn't seem to see Kimiko. "What did you get?"

"Just some bras," Allie said, opening her bag to show her and thinking, *Maybe she won't notice Kimiko.*

But Jack noticed her. "Hey, do you have a bike?" he asked, gesturing to Kimiko's Harley cap.

"Not yet," she replied, grinning a little awkwardly. She still didn't get what was going on with Allie.

"This is my friend Kimiko," Allie said. "This is Jenny and Jack. Remember the friend I told you about who has a motorcycle?"

"Oh, right. Cool. What kind do you have?" Kimiko felt a bit more at ease as she and Jack talked about motor-cycles, engine types, and cc's.

Meanwhile, Allie watched Jenny glance Kimiko over. Then Jenny turned and gave Allie a confused and kind of wounded look as if to say: *How come you never mentioned this person?*

Allie shifted nervously. What should she say? She wasn't sure why she felt so uneasy. When Kimiko and Jack paused in their conversation, she grabbed the oppor-tunity for Kimiko and her to break away.

"So, anyway . . . Well, we better go. See you at school."

"Nice meeting you," Jenny told Kimiko.

"Yeah, good to meet you," Jack said.

"Thanks, you too," Kimiko told them and followed Allie.

As they headed out of the store and into the mall, Allie let out a breath, feeling a sense of relief. "I'm glad you got a chance to meet Jack," she told Kimiko.

"Me too," Kimiko said. "But . . . can I ask you a

question? What was going on back there? It seemed like you tried to avoid them."

"Um . . ." Allie coiled a strand of hair between her fingers while she tried to sort out what to explain. "How about if we get a Coke or something?"

They returned to the food court, where Allie bought them sodas and they sat at a table near the one where they'd sat with Lance and Sergio.

"Remember that dream with a girl I told you about?" Allie said, sipping her Diet Coke.

"Yeah . . ." Kimiko nodded, trying to figure out what the dream might have to do with Jenny. "Was the girl Jenny?"

"No, no, no!" Allie had never felt anything like that toward Jenny. "But when I had the dream and told her about it, she had this kind of homophobic reaction. I know she likes Lance and she says she's okay with gay people, but she was kind of weirded out that I'd have a dream like that."

Kimiko sipped her root beer and mulled that over. The explanation didn't exactly make sense. "So you didn't want to see her because of me? But if she's okay with gay people, then why . . . ?"

"I don't know," Allie said. "I guess I just didn't want her to jump to conclusions about . . . you and me."

"Why would she think anything about you and me?" Kimiko asked. She couldn't imagine anyone thinking that she and Allie could possibly be a couple.

"I don't know," Allie repeated. "Look, I'm sorry about

this whole thing. I don't know what I was thinking."

Kimiko didn't know what to think either. Should she feel hurt that Allie didn't want people to think there was anything going on between them? Or should she feel flattered that Allie thought someone might imagine there was something going on?

"I really like you," Allie said. She put her hand lightly over Kimiko's and let it stay there for a moment before she pulled it away. "Okay?"

Before Kimiko knew it, the words popped out of her mouth: "I like you too, dude."

"Thanks." Allie said. She'd enjoyed hanging out with her. It felt different from being with other friends, although she couldn't describe exactly how—maybe because Kimiko was so different: boyish and yet a girl, Japanese and also American. Or maybe it had to do with the stirring she'd felt inside when she'd invited Kimiko to look at her in her bra.

"Want to walk some more?" Allie asked.

As they wandered around the mall, Kimiko wondered exactly what Allie had meant by "I really like you." And she realized she wasn't quite sure what she'd meant by "I like you too, dude."

"Who was your friend at the mall?" Jenny asked Allie at her locker Monday morning.

"Just a friend of a guy Lance went out with," Allie said, trying to sound nonchalant. "That's all." She'd known Jenny was bound to ask about Kimiko. But Allie wasn't ready to talk about what was going on and risk Jenny turning homophobe on her.

"When did you start hanging out with her?" Jenny asked.

"Just a couple of weeks ago."

"Are you still taking a break from Chip?" Jenny said.

"Yeah."

"Allie, is there something else you want to tell me?"

"No." Allie closed her locker, accidentally slamming the door. "Sorry."

"All right," Jenny said and offered a smile. "But if you do want to talk, you know I'll listen."

"Yeah, I know. Thanks," Allie said politely. Maybe Jenny wouldn't turn homophobe on her. After all, they weren't in middle school anymore. They'd both become a lot more mature since then and more comfortable with all sorts of issues.

As soon as Jenny left, Allie went to find Lance. "Can just you and I have lunch today?" she asked. "I really want to talk to you."

CHAPTER NINE

"I'm just not ready to talk to Jenny or anybody else about this yet," Allie complained to Lance over lunch at one of the school's outside picnic tables.

"Then don't," Lance soothed her. "You don't have to tell her."

"But I feel like I'm being a crappy friend. And what if she told someone else? You know how people would start to talk. Plus, it wouldn't be fair to Chip. I've got to sort things out with him first." Allie brought a hand to her forehead. "Sometimes this starts to feel too overwhelming. Can we change subjects? So, when are you going to call Sergio?"

"Why hasn't *he* called *me*?" Lance replied, pushing his french fries around his plate.

"Come on, babe," Allie said. "You can do this."

He knew she was right. That afternoon during swim practice, he psyched himself up with each lap.

When he got home, he started to dial Sergio's number. But then he decided to eat something first and made himself a PBJ sandwich. Then he checked to see if maybe

Sergio had e-mailed him. While he was online, Leo IM'd him for help with their English homework, and Lance did his own homework along with him. By the time he finished, his mom was calling him to dinner. After eating with his parents and helping to load the dishwasher, he got a text from Allie. *Have u called him?*

Too embarrassed to tell her no, he closed his bedroom door, deposited himself on the bed, and dialed.

"What up?" Sergio answered, sounding out of breath. "Hang on a sec." He turned the volume down on the video he was watching. "I'm learning some new steps to teach at Dance Club."

"Cool," Lance said, recalling his dream of one day dancing with a guy. "How's it going?"

"Good."

They both avoided discussing what they most wanted to find out. Instead they chatted about dancing, school, and friends, while Sergio continued to practice dance steps, excited that Lance had finally called. Maybe he wasn't dating that Jamal guy, after all.

"So, um, who was that guy you were with at the chick-flick the other night?"

"Jamal? He's a friend from school. We're on the swim team together."

"Only a friend?" Sergio asked.

The question took Lance by surprise. He hadn't considered that Sergio might think Jamal was a date. Lance didn't even know if Jamal was gay. One time he'd asked, but Jamal had merely mumbled, "I'm not sure yet" and changed the topic. After that, Lance had never brought it up again.

"Yeah, he's just a friend," Lance now told Sergio. "Why?"

"Just askin'," Sergio replied. He sounded a little jealous.

Lance gave a nervous giggle. He'd never experienced a guy feeling possessive of him. He kind of liked it.

"So, um, who was the girl you were with?" he asked Sergio.

"Serena? She's a new girl in Kimiko's creative writing class. . . . She asked me out."

"You mean . . . like on a date?" Lance nervously ran his hand across the bedspread. Even though he'd imagined that Serena might be a date, having it confirmed made him feel all jumbled and jealous and hurt.

"Yeah . . ." Sergio stopped dancing as he became aware of Lance turning quiet. "Since you didn't call me after our date, I didn't know if you were interested in going out again. I asked you out last time, so I figured it was your turn to call."

Lance took a breath, trying to clear his head. He felt angry with himself that he hadn't called sooner, like Allie had told him to.

"I'm sorry I didn't call," he told Sergio.

Sergio wiped the sweat from his brow. He felt bad hearing the regret in Lance's voice. "Well, I'm sorry I didn't call you, either."

"So, um . . ." Lance grabbed a tube of hand cream

from the nightstand and tossed it in the air. "Are you going out with her again?"

"No," Sergio said. "She doesn't really do it for me. Like in my car afterward, she was sort of waiting for me to make out with her. But I didn't want to, so I didn't."

Lance let out a sigh of relief. At least Sergio hadn't kissed the girl. That was some consolation. He recalled his own make-out session with Sergio and suddenly wanted to repeat it more than anything in the world.

"So, um . . ." Lance continued to nervously toss the hand cream. "Would you like to go out again?"

"Yeah . . . ," Sergio replied and started to dance again. "Would you?"

"Yeah," Lance said, sitting up in bed. They agreed on a date for dinner Saturday, and both were able to relax a little. After that they talked for a while about dancing, swimming, and working out. As soon as they got off the phone, Lance speed-dialed Allie and told her about the call.

"Super!" she exclaimed. "I knew you could do it."

"Yeah, but if he and I are going to keep dating, I think we should agree to be exclusive. Don't you think?"

"Babe, this is only your second date."

"But this feels so weird. If he wants to go out with other people, then I don't want to date him. He's got to decide on one or the other."

"Hmm . . ." Allie thought about that while she painted her toenails. " . . . The danger with an ultimatum like that is: What if he says no? Then what do you do?"

"Well, then I won't go out with him."

"Really?" Allie asked.

"I don't know," Lance admitted. "Why does dating have to be so complicated?"

Later that night when he took Rufus out for his bedtime walk, Lance's mind wandered back to thoughts of Sergio. Hopefully one day he'd be able to dance with him.

"I need the car for Saturday," Sergio told his parents at dinner the following night.

"Are you going out with Serena again?" his mom asked eagerly. "When do we get to meet her?"

"No, things didn't work out with her," Sergio said, slicing into his pork chop. "I'm going out with Lance instead."

His mom and dad stared across the table at each other, obviously wondering if he meant going out as friends or on a date. He decided to let them wonder.

Whether they figured it out or not, on Saturday his mom didn't give him any *churros* to take to Lance, and his dad didn't slip him a twenty.

"I wish my folks could be more like yours," he told Lance when he picked him up. Once again Lance's parents had invited Sergio to sit and chat. It felt so great to be treated as if dating a guy was the most natural thing in the world.

When Lance climbed into Sergio's car, he handed Sergio a bag of jelly beans tied to a little white teddy bear. "Here. I got this for you."

"Wow. Thanks, man." Sergio stared at the unexpected gift, recalling when Zelda had given him a teddy bear— a little brown one. After their breakup he'd buried the little bear inside his closet, along with a ukulele and the love notes she'd given him. He now propped Lance's bear onto the gearshift console between them and opened the jelly bean bag. "Want some?"

"Sure." Lance held out his hand but instead he got a jelly bean pressed into his mouth. "Thanks! So where are we going?"

"It's a surprise," Sergio said and drove to a nearby strip mall that Lance had never paid much attention to.

"Have you eaten here before?" Lance asked when they parked and walked toward a storefront restaurant called Zanzibar.

"Nope. A chick was handing out half-price coupons at the mall. It's Ethiopian. Where the hell *is* Ethiopia anyway?"

"Um, Africa." Lance had never eaten African food.

Inside, the restaurant had an herby spicy smell. Exotic music played over the speakers: drums, bells, flutes, and horns. . . . A tall dark-skinned waitress in a white sequined gown led them to a low, round woven-basket table. The place had no chairs; they had to sit on floor cushions.

"Are you okay?" Sergio asked, watching Lance shift and wobble on the floor cushion, trying to get comfortable. His long legs made it difficult.

"I'm good," Lance said, not wanting to be a spoilsport. He pointed at the trophy animal heads of antelope, oryx, gazelle, and ibex mounted on the walls. "Is that what we'll be eating?"

"Yeah." Sergio gave a laugh.

When the waitress returned to take their order, she recommended the "Sampler for Two" entrée and brought them a basin of water for washing their hands.

That's weird, Lance thought until he realized there wasn't any silverware. This was nothing like any restaurant he'd ever experienced before, not something he would've ever tried on his own.

The food arrived on a huge plate—a tray, really—that fit into the round tabletop. A big pancake-type thing was piled with six different-colored baby food–like mounds. A side plate contained more pancake thingies folded like napkins. The waitress explained how to tear off a piece of the spongy *injera* flatbread, grab some food with it, and pop it into their mouths.

"You can feed each other, too," she told them. "It's a tradition called *gursha*. We believe that those who eat from the same plate will never betray each other."

Sergio scooped up some food, leaned forward, and plopped it into Lance's mouth. His fingertips brushed Lance's lips. And as the waitress strode away, he licked his fingers one by one, grinning at Lance.

Lance blushed and glanced around to make sure nobody was watching. Sergio laughed.

Lance wasn't sure what he was eating, but maybe that was a good thing. Some of the food tasted sweet, some salty, and some was really spicy, but it all tasted delicious.

As they ate, Lance worked up his nerve for what he'd planned to talk to Sergio about. "So, um, I've been thinking . . ."

"Uh-oh," Sergio said, smiling out of one side of his mouth.

"If we're going to keep dating," Lance continued, trying to maintain his momentum, "I think it would be a good idea for us to be exclusive. You know: so that we don't have to worry about running into each other like at the movie theater and stuff. So, what do you think?"

Sergio thought for a moment. Although he liked Lance a lot, after Zelda, he wasn't ready to commit to anything serious so fast.

"This is only our second date, man. I'm not ready to be a couple."

Lance stared across the table, recalling what Allie had said about the danger of an ultimatum. So . . . now what? He didn't want to give up seeing Sergio. He enjoyed hanging out with him, he liked how Sergio got him to try new things, and it totally turned him on to watch him lick his fingers. He felt stupid for having brought this up. He wished he'd listened to Allie.

"Well, um, when do you think you'll be ready?" Lance asked.

"I don't know," Sergio said. "Can't we just chill and see how it goes?"

Lance shifted uncomfortably on the cushion, frustrated with the conversation, with Sergio, and most of all, with *himself*. "Okay," he said meekly.

"Great," Sergio said and hand-fed Lance another bite of some sweet orange goop.

Even though it felt hugely sexy to be fed like that, it also made Lance feel even more like a kid.

"Do you want to go somewhere?" Sergio asked when they went back outside to the car.

"Sure," Lance replied, still trying to sort out his jumbled feelings. "Like where?"

"I know a place," Sergio said. He drove them to a little poplar-lined lane he knew of alongside a nearby golf course. It was the make-out spot where Zelda had taken him to fool around. And as he now pulled beside the curb he wondered: How far would Lance be willing to go tonight?

He'd found that one difference between dating girls and guys was that a girl usually adjusted the speed of the relationship—pumping the brakes, shifting into neutral, or moving faster. But without a girl on the scene, it seemed like guys could go from zero to warp speed in seconds—almost as if on a dare as to who could get into whose pants faster.

Sergio shut the engine off and Lance glanced out the car windows.

It was Lance's first time to actually park in a lovers' lane. The scene seemed perfect: a latticework of tree branches blocked out the street lamps; the fairway stretched beyond them, still and quiet; and in the distance the moon shone nearly full. Without being aware of it, he began to hum "The Man in the Moon" from *Mame* and then caught himself. "Whoops. Sorry."

"I like it," Sergio said. Through the darkness, their gazes met and held. Sergio leaned across, and within seconds they were making out as feverishly as last time, lips pressing tight, tongues probing, hands moving across shoulders, sliding onto chests. . . .

As much as Sergio loved to explore the curvy softness of a girl, he loved just as much to touch the lean firmness of a guy. He ran his hands over Lance's abs, picturing the little bricks in the online photo, while Lance let his own hands grasp and squeeze Sergio's pecs. Sergio wasn't as built as Darrell, but he was definitely toned from working out. Lance's hands moved hungrily across his torso, wanting to feel every part of him. And sensing his desire, Sergio took hold of Lance's hand and moved it down from his chest to his zipper, giving him permission to explore there, too.

Lance's pulse throbbed in his temples. He was thrilled Sergio was letting him go there, but it was feeling too fast again, too soon. He forced himself to pull his hand away.

"Can we just stick to kissing tonight?"

"Sorry." Sergio backed off, feeling shot down. *This isn't going to work*, he thought. *He's just too inexperienced. I knew it wasn't going to work.*

Seeing Sergio's hurt look, Lance wished he hadn't stopped him. But he knew if he gave in to Sergio, he'd feel bad. And yet by not giving in to him, they *both* felt bad. Again he felt like he'd screwed up. He wished Allie were here to tell him what to do.

"I'm sorry," Lance mumbled. "It's just that . . . you're so much more experienced than me. . . . It kind of scares me."

"I didn't mean to scare you," Sergio said and remembered Kimiko telling him to go slow. "I just don't have as much self-control as you do."

"Well, I don't mean *scared*-scared," Lance explained. "I mean: I'm just not ready to do more yet."

"You're right," Sergio said. It wouldn't be a total hardship to stick to only kissing. Lance kissed better than any other guy Sergio had ever made out with, and as good as Zelda, if not better. "We should take things slow."

"You mean it?" Lance asked, trying to read Sergio's mood. "I mean: I know sometimes I can be too controlling. Allie can tell you that."

Sergio's feet bumped into something on the floor. During their passion the little bear had gotten knocked off the console between them. He picked it up now, brushed it off, and set it on the dashboard.

"Can we at least make out some more?"

"I'd like that," Lance said, relieved that Sergio wasn't dumping him for being an immature dweeb.

Then they were kissing again, but differently: calmer . . . more gently . . . each putting aside his cares about the future and just enjoying the moment.

On his drive toward home after dropping off Lance, Sergio phoned Kimiko and recapped the evening, telling her about the teddy bear: "No guy ever gave me anything like that before."

"Dude, I hear your defenses cracking."

"Whatever," Sergio mumbled. "Hey, remember how you said I should go slow? Well, I've decided you're right. I'm going to say no to sex for now—even if he throws himself at me."

"You really think you can do that?" Kimiko asked.

Her skepticism made him suddenly have second thoughts. "Well, like how *long* do you think I'll have to wait? And don't tell me till I'm married."

"No, just till you both feel ready. Since he's less experienced, let him set the pace. He obviously likes you. If you need to wait a month or two—"

"A *month or two*?" Sergio interrupted. "My balls will explode by then!"

"I doubt that," Kimiko said.

"You've got no idea how hard it is to be a guy," Sergio insisted. "You know how you sometimes complain about your little brother bossing you around and getting in your way? Imagine him living inside your pants twenty-four seven!"

Kimiko cringed. "Is it that bad?"

"Worse, man. At least you can get away from him."

Kimiko pondered that. For the moment at least, she was glad she wasn't a guy.

When Sergio got home, he brushed his teeth, undressed, and climbed into bed, bringing the little bear with him and wishing it were Lance between the sheets.

CHAPTER TEN

"You were right," Lance told Allie on their drive to church next morning. "I shouldn't have given him an ultimatum. He says he's not ready to be exclusive, so I'm stuck."

"You're not stuck," Allie argued. "If being exclusive is that important to you, then maybe he's not the right guy."

Lance thought about that for a second. "Guess what? I almost got into his pants! Actually, *he* almost put me into them. We came *this* close—" Lance gestured with his fingers "—but then I chickened out. I think it might've hurt his feelings. But we sort of talked about it. Why am I such a sex wuss?"

"You're not a sex wuss!" Allie reached across the car seat and squeezed his shoulder. "It's good to take things slow. How did he like the teddy bear?"

"I think he liked it." Lance told her about the Ethiopian restaurant and the rest of the date, circling back to almost getting into Sergio's pants. "But what if he gets bored waiting?"

"Well, if he can't wait, then he's not worth it."

"This is *so* mega-stressful," Lance said as they pulled into the church parking lot. Thank God he could get his nervous energy out by singing.

On Wednesday evening, Kimiko struggled with her math homework and tried to work up the courage to ask Allie for help.

"I'm too embarrassed," she told Sergio, "for her to find out how dense I am when it comes to numbers."

"Just call her," Sergio said, until finally she did.

"Hi," Allie answered. "How's it going?"

"Not so good—wrestling with math."

"Well, let me help," Allie offered. "Can you read me the problem?"

"Okay, but I need to warn you: I really, *really* suck seriously with numbers."

"Well, we can't all be good at everything. I could never write a poem like you. Let's hear the problem."

Kimiko read it to her and Allie walked her through the homework step by step.

"It seems like you're not sure of some basic stuff," Allie said. "If you want to hang out this weekend, I can go over it with you."

"That would be awesome," Kimiko replied, and they agreed to Friday night.

"Yee-hah!" Sergio cheered at lunch the next day when Kimiko told him about Allie's invitation. "Kimiko's got a da—"

She clapped her hand across his mouth. "It's not a date! She's going to help me with math. The dude is a mathlete."

But when she removed her hand, he persisted: "Well, you know the saying. Sex is like math: Add the bed, subtract the clothes, divide the legs, and hope you don't mult—"

She clamped her hand over his mouth again. "Can we change the subject, please?"

He nodded yes. But when she removed her hand, he revealed his crossed fingers. "So now pay attention to her body language. If she touches your *hand* that means she wants to be close friends. If she touches your *arm* that means she wants to be *more* than friends. And if she touches your *thigh* . . ."

"Paging new subject!" Kimiko stuffed her fingers in her ears, not wanting to hear any more of his goofy theories. "New subject, please pick up white courtesy phone!"

But Sergio leaned into her ear, his voice low and husky: ". . . It means she wants to get between your legs."

"Thanks a lot!" Kimiko said, pulling her fingers out of her ears. "As if I'm not already a nervous wreck."

"Oh, you'll be fine," Sergio said and laid his arm across her shoulder. "Hey, listen, I want to ask you: Would you mind if we made the homecoming dance a group thing and I asked Lance to go?" He'd previously asked Kimiko to go with him as friends.

"I don't mind," Kimiko said. She didn't particularly like to dance anyway.

"I'm not sure, though," Sergio continued. "He'll probably think it means we're engaged. . . . You want to know the strange thing? Even though I told him I'm not ready to be a couple, I don't really want to date anybody else. Isn't that weird?"

"No, dude. It sounds like you're going slow."

"I'm trying," he said with a sigh.

After school that day, they went together to the mall so she could help him pick out new shoes for the dance. Plus, he wanted to get an eyebrow piercing.

At the tattoo and piercing shop, the attendant had just about every appendage pierced, including both her ears (several times), nose, bottom lip, tongue, and right eyebrow.

"We have a twofer special today," she told Sergio. "Do you want to get something else done along with your eyebrow? Or your friend can get one too."

"Yeah, yeah!" he told Kimiko. "Do it! Do it!"

"No way," Kimiko said, recalling when she'd gotten her third and fourth ear piercings: Her mom had nearly had a heart attack. "My mom would completely kill me."

"Oh, come on," Sergio coaxed. "It'll look totally, completely, absolutely, hugely, orgasmically butch."

That convinced her. Afterward, Sergio draped his arm across her shoulder in front of the mirror while they each admired their shiny chrome eyebrow rings. She thought hers looked awesome; her mom was sure to have a meltdown.

Arriving at home, Kimiko pulled her cap down low

over her forehead and hurried to her room, postponing the inevitable. When dinnertime came, she steeled herself with several karate punches before heading downstairs. The house rule was that for meals she had to take her cap off.

"You got a ring on your eyebrow!" her brother announced the instant she pulled off her cap.

Her dad barely glanced at her and passed the broiled whitefish, but her mom's tone turned icy. "What have you done?"

Even though Kimiko didn't dare look at her, she could feel her mom's stare drilling into her.

"It's bad enough," her mom continued, "that you make yourself look like a boy. And now you make yourself even uglier?"

Kimiko sat silent, feeling as though a knife were slicing into her.

"It makes me ashamed to look at you. Take your food to your room."

Kimiko stood and put her cap back on. She carried her plate to the kitchen and left it there. She wasn't hungry. In her room, she turned some music on, curled onto the carpet, buried her head between her knees, and wiped her nose as she phoned Sergio.

"I told you she was going to kill me."

"Oh my god! Are you calling from the afterlife?"

Kimiko sniffled. "She said she's ashamed to look at me."

"And that's supposed to be a bad thing?" Sergio asked.

No matter how much Kimiko tried to feel sorry for herself, Sergio's comebacks were relentless. By the time she hung up, her mom's cuts no longer felt as devastating as before.

On Saturday afternoon, as Kimiko got ready to go to Allie's for dinner and math help, she stared at herself in the mirror, wondering if Allie would like the eyebrow ring.

"I love it!" Allie said the moment she saw Kimiko on the porch. "Here, let me take your backpack." She slung the pack onto her shoulder. "Come meet Mom and Dad."

In the kitchen, Allie's parents were preparing dinner while her little brother watched from a high chair. Both her dad and mom were as tall as Allie.

"You must be the famous Kimiko," Mr. MacBryde said, glancing up from the salad he was making.

"Am I famous?" Kimiko asked Allie, giving her a playful grin.

"Great to meet you," Mrs. MacBryde called over from the oven. "I hope Allie hasn't worn you out asking about Japan."

"No, I don't mind." Kimiko shrugged. "I like it."

"And this is Josh," Allie said, kissing her brother's forehead while he held a carrot out for Kimiko.

"Thanks, dude." Kimiko took the carrot, admiring his brilliant blue-green eyes, just like Allie's.

The girls prepared everyone's beverages, set the table, and talked about favorite foods until everything was ready.

"I like your hair," Allie said when Kimiko took her cap off at the dinner table.

"It's too stiff," Kimiko complained. "Zero body."

"No, I like it," Allie said, gently flicking her fingertips through it. Her touch made Kimiko recall Sergio's kooky theory about body language.

"So, is baseball still the big sport in Japan?" Mr. MacBryde asked, passing Kimiko a plate of salmon with dill sauce.

"Yeah," Kimiko said. "Also soccer and golf."

"What about those huge sumo wrestlers?" Mrs. MacBryde asked, handing her the buttered broccoli.

"Sometimes when we're in Tokyo," Kimiko replied, "my dad, my little brother, and I go to watch them."

"I'd love to see that," Allie said and proudly announced, "Kimiko does karate. She's a brown belt— that's almost like ninja level. And she's a poet. She writes wicked-amazing poems."

"Wow," Mrs. MacBryde said. "You're very talented."

Kimiko glanced down at her plate, feeling a little overwhelmed by all the praise and attention. "The salmon is delicious."

"Mom makes it really hard to stay thin," Allie said, grinning at Kimiko. "So you'd better not buy me any doughnuts!"

Kimiko immediately got the allusion to *Girl Panic*. "Oh, I brought you the third book."

"Awesome," Allie said and explained to her parents, "Kimiko turned me on to this really cool manga series."

Kimiko liked Allie's parents. They seemed as nice and pleasant as Allie. She felt comfortable with them. After finishing dinner, she put her cap back on.

"Oh, but you can see your eyes better without it," Allie said, pouting a little.

Kimiko thought for a moment and decided to pull the cap back off, wedging it into her pocket.

After they'd helped to load the dishwasher, Kimiko followed Allie to her room. A queen-size canopy bed was piled with ruffled pillows. The scent of potpourri lingered in the air. Plush little unicorns peered out from every corner. And on the bulletin board was Kimiko's kanji lettering.

"You still have it?" Kimiko said.

"Of course!" Allie set Kimiko's backpack on the loveseat. "What would you like to listen to? Do you like Alicia Keys?"

"Dude, I *love* Alicia Keys."

While Allie put the music on, Kimiko gazed around the room. On the nightstand was a photo of Allie and Chip. On a shelf alongside various Barbies were several books, including *The Complete Collected Poems of Maya Angelou.*

"Her poems are great, aren't they?" Kimiko said, flipping through the book.

"I *adore* her," Allie replied. "Who are your fave poets?"

"Wow, so many." Kimiko put the book back on the shelf. "Langston Hughes . . . Audre Lorde . . . Billy Collins . . . Edna Saint Vincent Millay . . . Walt Whitman . . ."

"Have a seat." Allie gestured to the loveseat. "So, was Whitman really gay?"

"Yeah," Kimiko said, sitting down. "A lot of poets are gay or bi."

"Edna Saint Vincent Millay?" Allie asked, taking a seat beside Kimiko.

"Yeah, she liked to be called Vincent."

"No way!" Allie pulled her lip gloss out of her jeans pocket. "That's funny."

"She was bi and had an open marriage," Kimiko explained, trying not to stare as Allie rolled the lip gloss across her shimmering lips. "She wrote these lines:

My candle burns at both ends
It will not last the night;
But ah, my foes, and oh, my friends—
It gives a lovely light!"

"I like that," Allie said, sliding her lip gloss back into her pocket. "Do you think it's about being bi?"

"It could be," Kimiko said. "Good poetry can have lots of meanings. It's all about metaphors."

"So do all bi people have open relationships?" Allie asked.

"I guess some do," Kimiko hadn't meant to get into the whole bi thing again. "Sergio doesn't. By the way, he said he'd be happy to talk to you."

"About what?" Allie asked.

"About being bi."

"Do you think I'm bi?" Allie asked, misunderstanding Kimiko's answer.

Kimiko realized her mistake. "I meant about *his* being bi. I told you that you should ask him about it, remember?"

"Oh, right." Nonetheless Allie's curiosity remained. "But do you think I might be bi?"

Kimiko tugged at her collar, growing warm. "I think only you can know that." She pulled the *Girl Panic* out of her backpack and handed it to Allie, eager to switch topics. "Here's Book Three."

"Wow, thanks!"

While Allie flipped through the manga, Kimiko gazed at her curly blond hair, wishing she could flick her fingers through it like Allie had done with hers.

"So, we're on chapter ten," Kimiko said, pulling out her algebra book. "Polynomials. I don't get it at all."

"Don't worry," Allie said, patting Kimiko's arm. "I know it can be confusing but we'll go slowly. Let me get my glasses."

While Allie walked to the desk, Kimiko's mind flashed back to Sergio's goofy theory again and what he'd said about touching someone's arm: Did Allie want to be *more* than friends?

She liked how Allie looked with glasses—they made her seem less perfect, a little flawed, kind of vulnerable, and even sexier. It took every brain cell of concentration for Kimiko to focus on math. It helped that Allie went back to some algebra basics like integers, variables, and radicals—stuff that Kimiko had never completely gotten. Allie patiently answered her questions and before Kimiko knew it, they were finishing the last problem in the chapter.

"Thank you so much!" Kimiko said, closing up her books.

"Anytime," Allie replied. "It makes me feel like I know something." She smiled at Kimiko. "So, when did you get the eyebrow ring? Did it hurt?"

"Only a little. It was sore for about an hour."

"Can I touch it?" Allie asked.

"Huh? Sure."

Allie lifted her fingertips and brushed them lightly across Kimiko's eyebrow. "Very cool."

"My mom didn't think so," Kimiko said. "She nearly killed me when she saw it, started yelling at me about how it's bad enough I wear guys' clothes, and why do I want to make myself uglier."

"*Uglier?*" Allie echoed. "You're not ugly." She let her fingertips drift from Kimiko's eyebrow down along her cheek. "You've got beautiful eyes, great skin, an adorable nose"—she playfully tapped the tip of it with her forefinger—"and all without makeup!" She brought her hand down. "It's sad she doesn't see that."

"She is who she is," Kimiko said and then grinned. "Sergio calls her Dragon Lady. She's usually nice but sometimes she practically breathes fire."

"Does she know you're lesbian?" Allie asked.

"How can she not know? She's not brainless. But

when it comes to anything personal, she's like: Don't ask, don't tell, don't want to know! That's like a house rule."

"Here it's the opposite," Allie said. "My parents want to be involved in like everything."

"You're lucky," Kimiko said. "Sometimes I want to shout, 'You know I'm gay! Why can't you just accept that?'"

"How do you think she'd react?" Allie said.

"She'd probably say I'm a bad daughter, bringing shame upon the family. In my culture that's the worst thing you can do: make them lose face. It's all about the family. To do what *you* want is to like betray the family."

"And your dad?" Allie asked.

"I think if I were my brother, he'd get upset. But with me he doesn't get very involved. I'm just a silly girl who likes to dress like a boy."

"Hmm," Allie said, thinking aloud. "I wonder how my folks would react if I told them I was bi or something. I don't think my mom would be angry. She'd probably just think it was a phase. I know she wants grandkids, but I could still have kids, right? And my dad just wants me to be happy. That's what he always says. He totally spoils me."

"My dad mostly just leaves me alone," Kimiko said.

"I wish things were better for you," Allie said, patting Kimiko's arm. "You deserve better."

"Thanks," Kimiko said and thought how one day when she had a girlfriend, she hoped it would be someone as caring and joy-inducing as Allie.

"That's a nice picture of you two." She gestured to the photo of Allie and Chip she'd noticed earlier.

"Thanks. I'm still trying to figure out our relationship."

"Anything new?" Kimiko asked.

"No, it's still on hold. Thanks again for helping me to sort it out." For an instant she tapped Kimiko's thigh, just above the kneecap. "I hope you don't mind."

"I don't mind," Kimiko squeaked, her mind flashing back once again to Sergio's goofy theory and what touching her leg meant. No way could it really be true. "It's getting late. I'd better go home."

Allie took her to say good night to her parents in the den, and afterward she walked Kimiko outside onto the porch. "Thanks for coming over."

"Thank *you* for your help, dude." Kimiko stared up at her and thought about the movies in which the couple kissed good night on the porch. *But this wasn't a date,* she reminded herself, *and she'd never be interested in kissing me.*

"It was fun," Allie replied. She gazed down at Kimiko and an unexpected thought popped into her mind: What would it feel like to kiss her? Would it feel any different from a boy? Would it feel as tingly as in her girl dream?

"Good night, dude," Kimiko said and stepped down onto the walkway, putting her cap on. Allie waved from the porch and watched her drive away.

Before Kimiko had gone even a block, she was on the phone with Sergio.

"Dude, where did you get that stuff about body language?"

"From one of my sister's magazines. Why?" Sergio put down the neck chain he was beading. "How far did Allie go?"

Kimiko tried to keep her concentration on the road. "First my arm—well, actually first my hair, then my face, then my arm, then . . . my thigh."

"Girl, she *wants* you!"

"Shush!" Kimiko fidgeted with her cap. "She helped me with math; that's all."

"And you helped her with . . . her sexuality?"

"She asked me if I think she's bi," Kimiko admitted.

"And did you say yes?"

"I don't know if she is!"

"There's one way to find out," Sergio said and started his singsong tease, "Kimiko is going to get laid, Kimiko is going to get—"

"I'm hanging up now," Kimiko interrupted him.

"Sweet Allie dreams," he said and returned to beading his necklace.

When Kimiko got home and undressed for bed, she pulled her baggy boy jeans off and gazed down at the spot just above the knee where Allie had tapped her. Kimiko pressed her fingertips against the skin, reliving the touch . . . and wished she'd had the nerve to touch her in return.

To Allie's surprise, that night she once again had a girl-on-girl dream—except this time the girl was Kimiko.

In the dream, Allie brushed her fingertips across Kimiko's face, down her cheeks to her lips. Then she leaned forward and kissed her—a kiss both tender and passionate . . . And her fingers slid gently beneath Kimiko's Harley jacket . . .

Then the dream changed. They were naked together. Allie's heart pounded with excitement. Her hands moved across Kimiko's skin. Her fingertips traced Kimiko's breasts and thighs. And she let Kimiko touch her, too; she wanted Kimiko to touch her everywhere.

Allie's heart beat so hard that it woke her. She lay in bed, catching her breath, her body pulsing, her thighs damp, half-expecting to see Kimiko beside her. The dream had seemed so real. In the darkness, she pushed the covers off and ran her hands across her moist body, feeling exhilarated, unsettled, and newly confused. For a long time she lay thinking about the dream, until at last she settled back to sleep.

"See, you're gay!" Lance exclaimed the next morning when Allie told him the dream. "Didn't I tell you?"

"Babe?" She gave him a stern look as they drove toward church. "Could you please not joke?"

"Sorry." He reached across the car seat and squeezed her hand. "So, um, what do you think the dream is about?"

"I don't know. Maybe I'm bi. Like yesterday, when Kimiko was leaving and we were on the porch, I thought: What would it feel like to kiss her?"

"Really?" Lance asked, turning into the church parking lot. "Would you actually do that?"

"I don't know. What if I didn't like it? Once we crossed that line, it would be hard to go back. I like her a lot, but I don't want to screw up our friendship."

Lance pulled into a parking space and turned the engine off, wishing he knew what to say to her. But he was having a hard enough time trying to navigate his relationship with Sergio.

Each day Lance looked forward to exchanging texts, IMs, or calls with Sergio, and he was thrilled when they did. But if he didn't hear from him or get a response, his insecurities crept back. Was Sergio dating somebody else? If so, who?

Then, just when Lance had become convinced that he'd been dumped for someone else, Sergio phoned.

"Hey, man," he told Lance on Tuesday. "Do you want to go to my school's homecoming dance with me?"

"What?" Lance fell back onto his bed, a little stunned. He'd never expected that question.

"A couple of guys went to the prom together last spring," Sergio said, "and it was no big deal. So, do you want to go? The dance is this Saturday."

"Um, yeah, sure," Lance said, trying to contain his excitement. Of course he wanted to go, but what did it mean?

"I'm *so* confused," he told Allie over the phone as soon as he'd hung up with Sergio. "He won't commit to being a couple but he invites me to homecoming? I don't get it."

"Well, just because you go with someone to home-coming doesn't necessarily mean you're a couple," Allie argued.

"Yeah, but this will be our third date. Doesn't that mean *something*?"

"Maybe . . . or maybe not. Why don't you just go with the flow and have fun?"

"I would if I knew what part to play: serious or just casual date."

All that night and into the next morning he tried to sort out his conflicting feelings.

"I've been thinking and thinking," he told Allie as they walked to their school GSA meeting at lunchtime. "Maybe I should take things to the next level with him. You know: move beyond making out."

"Why the switch?" Allie asked.

"Well . . . maybe if we went further, he'd be more willing to become a couple."

Allie turned and stared at him, pushing a stray curl behind her ear. "And what if he isn't more willing? Would you still want to move it to the next level?"

"I think so." Lance gave a bashful nod and lowered his voice to a whisper. "I keep thinking about him putting my hand on his zipper and what if—you know—I hadn't pulled away."

"Uh-huh . . ." Allie giggled. "I figured that was part of this."

"Maybe because he didn't jump my bones," Lance explained, "it makes me want to go further with him. Am I being flaky?"

"Makes sense to me," Allie said. "He respected you, so you trust him."

"Exactly!"

"Even if he's not ready to become a couple?" Allie asked as they got to the GSA meeting room.

"Yeah . . ." Lance sighed wistfully. "This sucks. It's like he wants one foot in and one foot out. Why can't he just commit?"

"I can drive this time," Lance offered the next time he

talked with Sergio on the phone. He was curious to meet Sergio's family, and if he were going to take things to the next level, he'd rather do it in his own car.

"Great," Sergio said. At dinner he told his parents he was going to the homecoming dance with Lance.

"He's the guy I mentioned last time," Sergio explained, figuring that if his mom and dad were going to make a stink about it, he'd rather they do it now. "You'll meet him when he comes to pick me up."

His mom glanced anxiously at his dad, and his dad stared back across the table at her. Neither of them protested, though his mom lit a new novena candle that night.

On Saturday afternoon, Allie went to Lance's to help him choose what to wear to the dance. While he pulled off one shirt and put on another, she glanced at his bare chest.

"What?" he asked, noticing.

"Nothing." She gave a little sigh and replaced his discarded shirts on hangers.

"How about this one?" He slid into a tight Lycra long-sleeve T. "Too gay?"

"Yeah." She cracked a grin. "But the shirt is nice."

"Ha ha." Lance tugged the shirt off. "So, should I take his mom flowers or something? Or would that seem like sucking up?"

"I think that would be sweet," Allie said. "But not roses, a simple mixed bunch."

"Good idea, thanks." He gave her a peck on the

cheek, and she made herself smile, wishing he got this excited when he went to dances with *her*.

On his way to Sergio's, he stopped at the supermarket and picked out an autumn-color bouquet of golden calendulas, sunflowers, and red daisies.

"These are for your mom," Lance whispered, when he got to Sergio's.

"Oh, man! She's going to love you." Sergio led him to the living room and introduced him to his parents.

"Nice to meet you," Mr. Martinez said, shaking hands. He was shorter than Sergio and had to tilt his head back to look up at Lance.

"Oh, thank you!" Mrs. Martinez said when Lance gave her the flowers. "You're very thoughtful." She asked Sergio to put them in water and invited Lance to take a seat. "I made some hot chocolate and dessert for you boys before you go."

While she and Sergio went to the kitchen, Lance was left alone with Mr. Martinez.

"Um, you have a nice house," Lance said.

"Thanks. Glad you like it." They sat silent for a moment until Mr. Martinez asked, "Do you play basketball?"

"Um, only in gym class. I'm on the swim team, though. Yeah, my school has a really good team. We always rank in the top five of the county. . . . I learned to swim when I was like three. I love it. . . . Um, what sports do you like?"

"Soccer," Mr. Martinez answered.

"I like soccer, too," Lance said, even though he'd hardly ever played and seldom watched it.

"Were you nice to him?" Sergio asked his dad when he and his mom returned with the hot chocolate and dessert.

"I'm always nice," his dad answered.

"Yeah, right." Sergio rolled his eyes.

"This is called *Tres Leches*," Mrs. Martinez said, passing Lance a slice of the sponge cake made with "three milks": condensed milk, evaporated milk, and cream.

"It's so frickin' good," Sergio told Lance. He handed his dad a bottle of lactose enzyme tablets, explaining to Lance, "My dad's intolerant."

"Too much milk," Mr. Martinez clarified, "doesn't agree with me."

"Doesn't the cake taste great?" Sergio asked as Lance took a bite.

"Delicioso," Lance replied. *"Gracias."*

"Ah! ¿Hablas español?" Mrs. Martinez asked.

"No, no, no." Lance gave a nervous laugh. "That's about all the Spanish I know."

While they ate, Mrs. Martinez led the conversation, asking Lance questions about his family and school, and relating stories about her own growing up in Mexico. Then she told him about how, when Sergio was little, he used to wear a Spider-Man costume under his clothes at school.

"Really?" Lance grinned at him.

"Yeah, to be ready if somebody needed rescuing," Sergio explained. Then he begged his mom, "Enough stories, okay?"

After they'd each eaten a second slice of cake, Sergio told Lance, "Come to my room. I want to give you something."

The first thing that struck Lance about Sergio's room was the wood shavings smell. The second thing was how messy the room was for a guy who dressed so neatly. CDs, video game cartridges, and magazines cluttered the dresser; a T-shirt hung off a bench-press set; and the teddy bear Lance had given him lay among the rumpled bedcovers. Lance almost felt like offering to straighten things for him.

"That's Elton," Sergio said, pointing to the guinea pig cage in the corner. "You can pet him if you want."

"Um, okay." While Lance stroked Elton through the wire, Sergio closed the bedroom door and brought Lance a gift-wrapped package. "Here, I got this for you."

"What is it?" Lance asked.

"Open it, man. You got me something last time, so I wanted to get you something."

Lance unwrapped a plush floppy-eared Irish setter. Its big brown eyes mirrored the warm fuzzy feeling that came over Lance. It was the first time a guy had ever given him something like that before. Even though Sergio said he wasn't ready to be a couple, it sure felt like they were becoming one.

"Thank—"

Before Lance could finish, Sergio had wrapped his arms around him, standing on tiptoe, and kissed him. For a moment, Lance closed his eyes and melted into the kiss—more ready than ever to take things to the next level—if only Sergio's parents weren't down the hall.

By the time they arrived at Liberty High, the homecoming dance was under way. Inside the cafeteria, the lights were turned down low, music was blaring, and about thirty couples were dancing—mostly Latino and African-American students—including one girl couple. Nobody seemed to notice the two girls, and Lance didn't pick up any homophobic vibes from anybody.

"'Sup, dudes?" Kimiko came over and fist-bumped Sergio and Lance. She was dressed like a total guy, with a man's suit, tie, and a fedora she'd borrowed from her dad in place of her usual baseball cap. She'd come to the dance with Serena, though only as friends.

"You remember Lance?" Sergio told Serena, while noticing that her low-cut purple dress totally embellished her boobs.

"Yeah, hi," Serena told Lance.

"Hi." Lance smiled cheerily, even though he felt a little awkward from knowing she wanted to make out with Sergio.

"How is Allie doing?" Kimiko asked Lance. "What's she up to tonight?"

"She's fine. Just hanging with friends, I think." He resisted mentioning Allie's sex dream about her.

"Well, let her know I said hi," Kimiko said.

While they were talking, Sergio spotted Zelda dancing with some black guy he'd never seen before. Was he the guy she'd dumped him for? Sergio shoved his fists into his pockets, suddenly feeling sulky and resentful. Zelda had never apologized for cheating on him. And yet he also felt a little embarrassed for her to see him at the dance with Lance, given how she'd argued that Sergio was gay, not bi.

But why should I feel embarrassed? Sergio thought. *It's none of her business.*

"That's Zelda." Sergio pointed her out to Lance. "My ex I told you about."

Lance looked over at the girl in the spaghetti-strap black dress. It felt weird to actually see a girl Sergio had had sex with. Lance still didn't totally get the bi thing, but at least it didn't trouble him as much as before.

"She looks nice," he said, not knowing what else to say.

"Want to dance?" Sergio asked. A Latin set had begun and he was eager to get his mind off Zelda.

"Okay," Lance said, "but I'm not exactly sure how to dance to this." The only time he'd danced with a guy before was briefly when learning a new step during studio lessons his mom had paid for.

"Just follow my lead," Sergio said, taking hold of his hand.

While Sergio led, Lance concentrated on following, ignoring a few people who stared. He wasn't sure if they were staring because he and Sergio were a guy-couple or because Sergio was such a good dancer.

"You dance great," Lance said as they slid into the rhythm. "Where did you learn?"

"Mostly from videos," Sergio said, bringing Lance in close, and then swinging him out.

"Really?" Lance loved the way Sergio's body moved.

"You're a good dancer too," Sergio said.

Occasionally his gaze happened across Zelda, and she smiled at him as if totally unashamed to be seen with the guy she'd ditched him for.

"How's it going?" she shouted when she got close enough to talk over the music.

"Good," he replied, not really wanting to talk with her.

"Glad to hear that," she yelled, sounding as though she meant it.

And suddenly he was the one who felt ashamed for still harboring a grudge against her. Yeah, it would be nice if she'd apologize for cheating on him. But apparently she wasn't going to, so why bother hanging on to the resentment?

"How's it going with you?" he shouted back to her.

"Good!" she said.

"Glad to hear that, too," he replied and meant it. When the music changed to a slow song, he nestled into Lance's arms, no longer embarrassed at all. It excited him to feel the muscles of Lance's back and shoulders. And he felt genuinely happy that things had ended with Zelda so that he could be with him.

When the song ended, they met up with Kimiko and Serena at the refreshment counter. The four of them talked about differences between Latino and American pop music, and commented on people dancing, comparing different steps until Serena asked Lance, "Mind if I steal your partner for a bit?"

"Um, if you promise to give him back," Lance said, half-grinning and half-serious.

Watching them dance together, he was totally impressed. They moved a lot better than Sergio and he did, almost like an ace dance team.

When the set changed to a fast rock song, some curly-haired guy began to dance with both Sergio and Serena in a threesome.

"Who is he?" Lance asked Kimiko.

"A guy Sergio went out with."

"Um, yeah?" Lance's stomach clenched with a twinge of jealousy and his anxiety returned. Was Sergio going out with the guy *now*?

When Sergio returned, Lance handed him a cup of ice water to help him cool down and asked, "So, um, is he your ex too?"

"Hector? Not exactly," Sergio said, guzzling the water down. "We only made out a couple of times. He was too possessive."

Lance cringed, recalling Darrell once telling him he was too clingy. He knew he should stop this conversation. But he couldn't.

"Um, can I ask you something? Like, are you going out with anyone else now?"

Sergio thought about the question and tossed his empty cup aside. "Why do you want to know that?"

Lance gave a shrug. "I guess I'd like to know who my competition is."

Sergio glanced across the dance floor, debating how to

respond. Even though he wasn't dating anybody besides Lance, the conversation was making him uneasy.

"I don't think it's a good idea for us to talk about this," he told Lance. "It feels like you're trying to pin me down again. I told you I'm not ready to be a couple."

"So then why did you invite me to homecoming?"

"Because I wanted you to come with me. I thought it would be fun."

Lance gritted his teeth, remembering Allie telling him to "just go with the flow and have fun." If only it were that easy. He watched the dancers and brooded.

"You want to dance some more?" Sergio asked.

"Sure," Lance said, hoping to burn off his frustration. It helped when the DJ played "Electricity" from *Billy Elliot the Musical*, one of Lance's favorites. The song seemed to express how scared, mixed-up, and mad he felt. As he danced and sang along, he gradually found himself also uncontrollably happy to be with Sergio . . . and once again eager to take things to the next level.

"You want to go to that place you took me to last time?" he asked Sergio after they'd said good night to Kimiko and Serena and were leaving the dance.

"You bet," Sergio answered, knowing Lance meant the little lane where they'd made out. He was glad that Lance had gotten over his funk about dating and gave him directions back to where they'd parked beneath the poplar trees.

Sergio cracked the window a little, still feeling warm from dancing. Across the car, Lance smelled faintly of sweat and FIERCE cologne—a good smell. . . . Masculine . . . Sexy . . . Sergio leaned over, kissed him, and within seconds they were all over each other: arms circling, tongues in each other's mouths, hearts pounding.

Lance's heartbeat throbbed with anticipation for Sergio to move his hand back to his zipper like last time.

But Sergio didn't. He was determined to let Lance set the pace, like Kimiko had suggested. He was sort of enjoying the thrill of wanting but waiting—at least for now.

This time it was Lance who felt impatient, even though he couldn't blame Sergio for not making the move. After getting shot down last time, why would Sergio set himself up again? Lance could, of course, make the move himself, but that felt so bold. Instead, he began to nudge Sergio's hand down toward his pants, hoping Sergio would get the hint.

At first, Sergio wasn't sure what was going on, except that his hand was being bumped inch by inch down Lance's torso . . . until it landed on his zipper.

I guess we're moving on, Sergio thought, and the excitement of that possibility overcame the thrill of waiting. Figuring he wouldn't get slammed again, he placed Lance's hand on his zipper too. And sure enough, Lance kept it there this time; he didn't pull away.

As they made out ever more feverishly, their hands moved and rubbed across the front of each other's jeans. Fingers tested zippers. Pants were fumbled open.

Lance felt about to explode as Sergio slid his hand inside, grabbed hold of him, and—

"Ahhh!" Lance gasped in climax, as alternating waves of ecstasy and embarrassment surged through him. How had it happened so fast?

"Sorry, sorry," he whispered. But before he could utter another word, Sergio was prompting his hand and—

"Whoa!" Suddenly it was Sergio who was gasping, almost as quick, giving Lance some consolation.

"That was awesome," Sergio whispered, catching his breath, overjoyed that he hadn't had to wait two months.

"It wasn't too fast?" Lance asked.

"I guess I was excited," Sergio said and leaned his head back on the headrest.

"Yeah, me too," Lance said. Without realizing it, he began to hum. He felt so glad they'd moved to the next level. More than just glad—exuberant. In spite of his concerns about Sergio, he felt more connected to him than he ever had to Darrell. And unlike his sex attempts with Darrell, this time he felt like singing.

As soon as Lance got home, he called Allie. "We had hand sex!" he whispered into the phone even though his bedroom door was closed.

"Woo-hoo!" She giggled, picturing the scene in her mind.

"Mega-woo-hoo!" Lance replied. He'd never understood why Allie got so excited hearing about guy-on-guy action, but he didn't mind.

"I'm not washing my hand for a year," he continued, as he pulled his shoes off and told her about the homecoming dance and seeing Zelda. "It felt a little weird to see a girl he'd actually had full-on sex with. But I think I'm mostly over the bi thing. There was also a guy he'd gone out with. So, like, do you think I'm possessive?"

"Not with me," Allie said, half-jokingly. "Do you mean with Sergio? Hmm. I wouldn't say *possessive*—more like *unsure . . . cautious . . .*"

"Well, wouldn't you be?" Lance asked. "We had hand sex. To me that means we're a couple. Don't you think so? And he gave me this really cute plush puppy. . . . Hey, by the way, Kimiko said to say hi. She looked really cute wearing a guy's suit and tie and a hat."

"She's so adorable with her whole boyish thing," Allie said and began to brush her hair.

"So, how was your evening?" Lance asked, stroking the plush Irish setter.

Allie told him she'd hung out with Jenny, Jack, and Leo, another friend from their group. "He asked if I'm still going out with Chip. Jenny told me afterward that Leo said he wants to go out with me if I'm not seeing Chip anymore."

"So, do you want to go out with Leo?" Lance asked.

"No. I like him as a friend, but not more than that. Besides, I've been thinking: Remember I told you about the last time I saw Kimiko and how I wondered what it would feel like to kiss her?"

"Are you going to try it?" Lance asked, sitting up in bed.

"I don't know," Allie said, continuing to brush her hair. "What if I'm *not* bi? I don't want to ruin my friendship with her. I really, really like her."

"Well . . ." Lance wiggled his toes, sore from dancing. "Maybe you should talk with her about it."

"But what would I say?" Allie asked.

"Tell her what you just told me," Lance suggested. "That you like her but you're scared to mess up your friendship."

After thinking about that a moment, Allie set her brush aside. "I wonder if Kimiko has ever gone out with anyone. She's never mentioned it. Wait, that's not true. Once she said she had zero experience with relationships. I should ask her. She probably thinks I'm a mess always asking her questions about stuff."

"You're not a mess," Lance consoled her. "At least no more than me."

They talked for a while longer before hanging up. Then Allie climbed into bed and read Book Three of *Girl Panic*. There was a lot more girl/girl kissing than in the first two, but none of the full-on sex action that so many boy/boy mangas had. She kind of wished there was.

TWELVE

One evening the week after homecoming, Kimiko planted herself on her bedroom carpet to write a poem she'd been putting off, due the next day for her creative writing class. When she opened her poetry notebook, the daisy from Allie's car dashboard fell out onto her lap.

Kimiko had forgotten she'd saved the flower there, pressed between the pages. She brought it to her face and inhaled the faint scent, picturing Allie in her VW bug, singing to sixties songs, her blond curls whipping in the open-window breeze.

Alegría, Kimiko wrote, *the Spanish word for "joy."*

She stared at the words, chewed on her pen, and wondered: What was Allie doing now? Homework? Having dinner with her family? Playing with her little brother?

She thought about the first time she'd met Allie and jotted down: *How can you resist joy when it bounds toward you, stumbling over its outsize front paws?*

Kimiko read over the words and wanted to crumple the page up, start over. Then she recalled Allie telling her, "You write beautifully."

She made herself continue to write another line, then another. During the rest of the evening, she pieced together words and images, inserting lines and crossing them out, shifting stanzas back and forth.

A little before midnight, her mom tapped on the door. "It's late, Miko," she said softly. After several days of sulking, her mom had gradually gotten over her anger about the eyebrow ring.

"Okay, I'll go to sleep in a minute," Kimiko said, honestly intending to. But then she started to fuss with the words again, and the next time she looked at the clock, it was past one. Feeling spent and ready to throw the poem out, she put her pen down and crawled into bed. It seemed as if she'd barely fallen asleep when she awoke to the sound of her mom's voice again.

"Wake up, Miko." She gently shook her shoulder. Sunshine was splashing in the window. "You're going to be late for school. What time did you go to sleep?"

"I don't remember." Kimiko yawned, stumbling out of bed, and got ready.

During homeroom, she copied her last night's poem onto a clean sheet of paper, tinkering with a few more words, still unsatisfied with it.

"I think you should read it at the poetry open mike," Ms. Swann said, handing it back the next day.

The open mike was held for all the county high schools once each semester—for anybody who wanted to recite or read an original poem in front of a live audience of students, teachers, friends, and family.

"Really?" Kimiko asked. "Do I have to?"

Getting in front of the mike could sometimes be fun but was already nerve-racking.

"You don't *have* to," Ms. Swann told Kimiko, "but I encourage you to."

To Kimiko, that sounded pretty much like she had to; she didn't want to disappoint Ms. Swann.

"All right." Kimiko said, and made herself smile.

"Can I come?" Allie asked when Kimiko called and told her about the open mike. "I'd love to hear more of your poetry."

Kimiko turned silent, realizing her mistake. She shouldn't have mentioned the event. If Allie came, would she figure out the poem was about her?

"The poem's not very good," she told Allie.

"I bet it's great—otherwise why would your teacher want you to read it?"

Kimiko tried to think of a way out of it. "She asked other people too, not just me. It can be a pretty boring event. I doubt you'd enjoy it."

"I'd like to try it," Allie said. "Unless you don't want me to come."

"Well . . ." Seeing no escape, Kimiko forced the words out. ". . . If you really want to come . . ."

The instant they'd finished talking, she speed-dialed Sergio.

"Dude! I think I really-really stuck my foot in it this time. She's sure to realize the poem is about her."

"Can't you just read a different poem?" Sergio suggested.

"No, I can't. Ms. Swann told me to read that one. What am I going to do?"

"Admit you've got a crush on her, I guess."

"You're a big help," Kimiko said, wishing she'd crumpled up the poem when she'd had the chance.

On Friday evening, Allie picked Kimiko up after dinner, and while Allie talked with Kimiko's mom, Kimiko sat on her hands, trying to keep still.

The open mike took place at a neighboring high school. Threading her way through the crowd in the lobby, Kimiko found Ms. Swann sitting at the registration table.

"I already put your name on the list," she told Kimiko. "I figured you'd want to get it over with. You're number five."

"Thanks," Kimiko said. After introducing Allie, they went inside the auditorium and took a couple of seats by the aisle.

"Wow, there are a lot of people," Allie said as they sat down. "Are you nervous?"

"Um, yeah," Kimiko replied. She left out that her nervousness largely had to do with Allie's being there.

The MC, a teacher with a thin little mustache, welcomed everybody and introduced the first reader, a boy whose poem was a hip-pop in-your-face rap about cars and girls. The boy punctuated the words with vocal effects of car engines and police sirens. When he finished, everyone clapped and cheered, and he clasped his fists in the air like some prizefighter.

Next up was a grinning heavyset girl who recited from memory a racy, funny metaphorical poem that compared making love and baking bread, playing with the words needing and kneading.

Following her, a boy with wraparound Bono glasses gave a dramatic reading of his bitter breakup poem, going from angry shouts to voice-cracking sniffles.

As reader number four walked up to the mike, Kimiko clutched her own poem tightly in her fist. She couldn't even hear the boy reading, only her own nervous heartbeat.

"Next," the MC announced, "is Kimiko Kawabata from Liberty High. Come on up, Kimiko."

"Break a leg," Allie whispered, pressing Kimiko's hand.

That would be one way out of this, Kimiko thought. She walked up onto the stage to the microphone and unfolded the sweat-soaked sheet of paper. Her fingers were trembling. She cleared her throat and pulled her cap low over her forehead to avoid looking out at the audience. If she saw Allie, she'd lose her nerve altogether.

"Alegría," she began, her voice quivering. "Spanish for 'Joy.'"

Allie shifted in her seat. Was the poem related to her? That Kimiko might write about her had never crossed Allie's mind. Why would Kimiko write about *her*?

"How can you resist joy," Kimiko continued,

"when it comes bounding toward you
stumbling over its outsized front paws

and leaps into your lap, its wet nose tickling your face
while you try to hold it down?"

Ugh, what a stupid image! Kimiko cringed. *Why did
Ms. Swann make me read this?* She had to push herself to
continue:

"Joy is the discovery that your parents are going away
for the weekend,
     and so you invite a friend over—only one, or maybe
two—
     but they invite their friends,
     and soon you're having the most amazing party ever.
     You know it's going to end badly,
     you're going to be grounded for life. But for now,
     you've never felt so alive."

Allie listened intently, trying to figure out the connection between her and the words Kimiko was reading.
Maybe the poem wasn't about her. Meanwhile Kimiko
made herself go on:

"Joy is the wave that swells in your chest and crashes
to shore,
     leaving a trail of foam that blows down the lonely
beach
     and you bound after it, arms outstretched.
     It's the music in you
     while you sing out the car window with the wind
rushing in.

It's the angel flying into the sky, taking you with her.

And you follow, even though you know the heartbreak to come.

It's the wish that maybe came true,
because what you wished for
was joy."

Kimiko let out a breath, relieved to have reached the end. The audience applauded as she folded the poem up and stepped away from the mike. She shuffled up the aisle, wanting to continue walking out of the auditorium and into the street. When she got back to her seat, she felt too embarrassed to look at Allie.

"It was beautiful," Allie whispered.

Kimiko glanced at her. She didn't seem shocked or horrified. She was smiling. Didn't she realize the poem was about her? Why wasn't she freaked out?

Kimiko leaned back in her seat, too confused to even hear the next poem or the one after.

"That was a lot of fun," Allie said, when the last poet had finished. "I loved, loved, loved your poem."

"Thanks," Kimiko said, both thrilled and a little worried. What exactly did Allie mean? That she liked the poem itself—or that she knew what was behind it?

They told Ms. Swann good-bye and after leaving the school, they drove to a nearby coffee shop to hang out. Kimiko got some hot mint herbal tea to help settle down. Allie got a latte.

While Kimiko regrouped, Allie said which poems

she'd liked best. Kimiko barely remembered any of them; she'd been so preoccupied with her own. But Allie's memory was amazing. She giggled about the one that compared making love and baking bread. Then she turned serious, saying how she'd loved the images in Kimiko's poem.

"Thanks," Kimiko told her, feeling warm from the tea and nervousness.

"I want to ask you something," Allie said. "I know you told me you don't have any experience with relationships but . . . have you ever, like, dated a girl?"

Kimiko swallowed the lump in her throat. "No."

"Have you ever *wanted* to be in a relationship?" Allie probed further.

"Sure, I guess. I mean, doesn't everybody?"

"Then how come you haven't?" Allie asked.

Kimiko fidgeted with her cap, sliding the bill forward and back. Why was Allie asking all this? *Is she just interested out of curiosity?* Kimiko wondered. *Or is she asking to find out if I'd be interested in her?* No, that couldn't possibly be it.

"I guess it just hasn't worked out," Kimiko said. "Who would want to be my girlfriend? And if my mom found out, she'd really flip."

Allie thought about that. "But you said she got over the eyebrow ring, right? Maybe if she liked the person you liked, she'd come around."

Kimiko sipped what was left of her tea. This conversation was making her more and more anxious. "You want something else to drink?"

"No, thanks." Allie noticed Kimiko's fidgetiness and wished she could do something to help her, but didn't know what. "Would *you* like something else?"

"No, I'm fine. Fine."

On the drive back to Kimiko's house, Allie thought about the things that Kimiko had said. It sounded like maybe she didn't want a relationship. Or was she just too scared of her mom?

Kimiko put on some Peter, Paul, and Mary songs and rolled down her window to sing along. The fresh air helped her relax a little. She took off her cap to keep it from blowing away, and when they pulled up in front of her house, she left it off.

"I always have a cool time with you," Allie said, shutting off the motor.

"I do, too," Kimiko said. "I mean with you." She peered across the car seat at Allie, feeling nearly as nervous as when she'd read her poem. "You know my poem was about you, right?"

"Yeah." A little smile played across Allie's mouth. "I mean, I thought maybe it was."

"And it doesn't bother you?"

"Bother me?" Allie gave her a blank look. "No. I'm kind of flattered. I mean, it's the first time anybody has ever written a poem because of me."

Kimiko's stomach gave a flutter and her face grew warm. She wished something would happen, although she didn't know what. She only knew that something had to happen soon or she would surely die from nerves.

From across the car, Allie stared at her, wondering once again what it would feel like to kiss her.

"I like you a lot," she told Kimiko and took hold of her hand.

Kimiko's pulse nearly stopped. "I like you a lot too."

"I'm afraid to screw it up," Allie continued, recalling her conversation with Lance.

"Screw what up?" Kimiko asked.

"Us," Allie said. She braced herself on the steering wheel and drew a deep breath. "Have you ever kissed a girl?"

Kimiko shifted in her seat, speechless, while a thousand thoughts collided in her mind. Did Allie want to kiss her? Why would she? What if they did kiss? What would happen to their friendship? Maybe she'd heard wrong, just imagined it.

"What?" she asked Allie, just to be sure.

"Did you ever kiss a girl?" Allie reiterated. There was no mistaking the question.

"Once . . . ," Kimiko said softly, remembering her experience with Hannah. "In seventh grade . . . during this sleepover at a friend's. We were listening to some boy bands. I began to play air guitar, and she pretended to be like my adoring groupie . . . and suddenly we—you know—kissed. That was it."

"What was it like?" Allie asked, eager to hear more.

"It was good," Kimiko said and thought: *Glorious would be a better adjective*. "I wanted it to happen again after that night . . . but it never did. I guess she didn't like it as much as I did."

Allie nodded for Kimiko to go on. She wanted to hear more about the kiss, although she wasn't sure what. But her body seemed to know: She gazed into Kimiko's eyes, her breath coming faster. Then she leaned forward, tilted her head a quarter turn, and rested her lips on Kimiko's.

Kimiko closed her eyes. Her stomach wobbled as though on a roller coaster. Her entire body tingled and sparked as she gently kissed back. Was this really happening?

Allie tried to make her heart slow down. The kiss felt more tender than any boy's. Kimiko's cheeks smelled fresher. Her breath tasted clean and sweet like mint and honey. And although it felt a little naughty to slide her tongue between Kimiko's lips, it felt so natural. Magical. Good. . . . So, did this prove she was bi?

"Wow," she said when she finally pulled away.

Kimiko tasted Allie's cherry-flavored lip gloss on her lips and stared into her eyes, trying to figure out what had just happened. "Why did you do that?"

Allie withered a little. Why was Kimiko asking that? Hadn't she wanted to kiss? It felt like she had.

"I did it because I like you," Allie said simply.

The answer confused Kimiko. Just because they liked each other didn't mean they should kiss each other— unless Allie meant *like* as in "more than a friend." But how could anybody as good-looking, confident, and awesome as Allie possibly mean that?

"What's wrong?" Allie asked. Obviously something was wrong.

"Dude, we shouldn't have done that," Kimiko said, putting her cap back on.

"Why?" Allie insisted.

"Because . . ." Kimiko struggled to explain the pandemonium of feelings swirling inside her. "Look at you—and look at me."

"What?" Allie asked. Was it because of her height?

"This can't work," Kimiko said. "We should just be friends and leave it at that."

"O . . . kay . . . ," Allie said, although she actually felt more confused than okay. This was nothing like any other reaction she'd ever had to a kiss. What was going on? "I'm sorry," she told Kimiko.

"No, *I'm* sorry," Kimiko said. "I didn't mean to get so upset. We'll just be friends, okay?"

"Sure," Allie replied. "If that's what you want."

Kimiko wasn't sure what she wanted other than to kiss her again. "I think I better go," she said, grabbing the door handle. She climbed from the car, closed the door, took a step, but then turned around and opened it again. "Thanks!"

"Yeah," Allie said, feeling kind of rattled, and watched Kimiko skitter into the house.

"How was the poetry reading?" Kimiko's mom asked from the sofa where she was watching the Japanese channel with Kimiko's dad.

"Fine!" Kimiko said as she hurried past them.

"Miko!" her mom called. "What's the matter?"

"Nothing!" Kimiko shouted back. "Just leave me alone!" She closed her bedroom door, brought her fingers to her forehead, and tried to calm down. Then she pulled out her cell and phoned Sergio. "Dude! We kissed!"

"No way!" he answered, pausing the DVD he was watching.

"Way!" Kimiko said, kicking off her shoes.

"You don't sound exactly ecstatic," Sergio said. "What's the matter?"

"We shouldn't have—that's what."

"Why?" Sergio twirled the TV remote between his fingers.

"Because she's out of my league."

"Well," Sergio argued, "apparently she doesn't think so."

"Plus," Kimiko went on, ignoring his response, "she's been dating a *guy,* with whom she's still half-involved. There's no way we can have a relationship—and now we can't be friends, either."

"Why not?"

"Because I like her too much. And we kissed. We crossed the line!"

"Well then, how about friends with benefits?"

"Dude, don't joke about this."

"I'm not; I'm just being practical. If there's too much mojo between you, then—"

"I don't want to be friends with benefits," Kimiko cut him off.

"So what *do* you want?" Sergio asked and tossed the remote aside.

"I don't know." Kimiko tugged her cap off, frustrated. "And you're not helping!"

"Well, what am I supposed to say?" Sergio fired back. "That, yeah, you shouldn't have kissed? You're a bad, bad girl—go to your room? Come on, what's the big deal?"

"You just don't get it," Kimiko said, her voice breaking. "I'm hanging up now."

"Hello?" Sergio said and realized she was gone. It was hardly the first time she'd hung up on him. Right away, he dialed her back. No answer. When he tried a second time, she'd turned her phone off, and his call went straight to voice mail.

"Would you stop being such a drama diva?" he grumbled. "You guys wanted to kiss, so you did. Why make it into a disaster?"

The moment he hung up, he regretted having left the message. He should've just let her cool off. But it seemed obvious that she and Allie were hot for each other. Why couldn't Kimiko just let herself enjoy it?

Maybe he should call her back and apologize for the "friends with benefits" suggestion. Or maybe he should just try to phone her again tomorrow. Hopefully she'd be over it by then.

CHAPTER THIRTEEN

"I think I screwed up," Allie told Lance over the phone as she drove away from Kimiko's.

"What happened?" Lance asked, pausing in the middle of walking Rufus.

"Are you sitting down?" Allie asked.

Lance dropped down onto the curb. "Now I am."

Allie took a breath and whispered, "I kissed her."

"Are you serious?" Lance leaped up from the curb.

"I kid you not."

"This is huge!" Lance exclaimed. "Did you like it?"

"Yeah. *Totally*." Allie's mind drifted back to the kiss. "She kisses really, really good. I think girls kiss different from boys. Softer. More tender."

"So are you guys like dating now?" Lance asked.

"No." Allie let out an audible sigh. "Things got sort of weird."

"Weird? How?"

"Hold on. I think I'd better pull over. I'm kind of rattled by it." Allie drove the car to the curb of a side street and stopped so she could concentrate. "Okay . . .

So, like, first of all she said she's not dating anyone. And you know the poem she read tonight? It was about me. So I know she likes me. And it seemed like she liked kissing. I mean, she kissed me back like she meant it. But then she said she wants to just be friends. She doesn't think she and I can work."

"Why not?"

"I'm not sure. I think she's got self-image issues."

"But she's so cute," Lance argued.

"Yeah, but I guess she doesn't think so. I shouldn't have kissed her, should I? I hope I didn't screw everything up. Do you think I screwed up?"

"No, it seemed kind of inevitable. Kissing, I mean."

"You think so?" The thought cheered her. "So do you think that this plus the two girl-dreams prove I'm bi?"

"Um, I don't know." Now that Allie had actually kissed a girl he no longer felt like leaping to the conclusion that she was a latent lesbian. Maybe she truly was bi like Sergio.

"So what are you going to do?" Lance asked.

"I'm not sure." Allie pulled away from the curb and began to drive toward home again. "I really like her and she said she likes me. I'm just not used to being the pursuer—especially with a girl. This all feels so new. Any ideas?"

"Hmm . . ." Lance wanted to be helpful but he was hardly an expert at pursuing either—and definitely not with a girl. "Maybe send her a text? So she knows you're thinking of her?"

"That's good. I like that: thoughtful but not pushy. Great idea! Can you hold on again?" She pulled the car over to the curb once more and texted Kimiko: *Thinking of u. Hope u r ok. Look fwd to c u again soon!*

While waiting and hoping to hear back from Kimiko, she resumed her drive and conversation with Lance. "So, how was your evening? I haven't let you talk."

"Dull compared to yours." As he headed home with Rufus, he told her he'd gone to Jamal's to play some games. "That's all."

"So, do you think she'll text me back?" Allie asked, returning the conversation to Kimiko. Allie continued to talk for a half hour while she arrived at home, went inside, and got ready for bed, until she finally calmed down enough to go to sleep.

When Lance climbed into bed, he lay awake for a while, absorbing the thought that his best straight friend from ever since first grade had actually kissed a girl. Was the whole world going bi?

"Did Allie tell you about the smooch?" Sergio asked Lance over the phone the next morning.

"Yeah." Lance had just showered and gone back to his room to get dressed.

"So, what do you think?" Sergio was still in bed, just waking up.

"Um, I don't know." Lance wedged the phone beneath his ear and stepped into his jeans. He felt a little uneasy about repeating the stuff that Allie had confided in him.

"Did Allie like it?" Sergio insisted, scooting up on his pillows.

"Yeah . . . Did Kimiko like it?"

"Yeah." Sergio didn't feel as concerned about repeating the things that Kimiko had confided. He was no good at keeping secrets and he hoped that sharing Kimiko's stuff might help bring her and Allie together. "But she's scared because she's never dated anybody and thinks Allie is out of her league. Plus she's worried about Allie still being half-involved with that guy. But at the same time, she also thinks there's too much mojo between them to just be friends."

"So is she going to want to date Allie?" Lance asked as he pulled a pair of socks on.

"I don't know. She hung up on me."

"How come?" Lance stood and brushed his hair in the mirror.

"Because I said that if they're too hot for each other to just be friends, and she's too scared to date, then maybe they should be friends with benefits."

Lance set his hairbrush down, feeling a little alarmed. Although he knew of schoolmates who had friends with benefits, he would've never considered that possibility— and as far as he knew, neither would Allie. "Does Kimiko want to be friends with benefits?"

"No. That's why she got mad at me. I was just trying to be practical."

Lance had never thought of FWBs as "practical." The idea of sex with a person without being a couple made him uneasy, especially since he'd had hand sex with Sergio while they weren't officially a couple.

"So, um . . . ," he asked cautiously. "Do you think of *us* as friends with benefits?"

"No, man! Why would you ask that?"

"Well, because we—you know—fooled around even though you said you're not ready to be a couple. So like . . . what exactly does that make us?"

The line went silent for a moment while Sergio shifted beneath his sheets, thinking about the question. He'd tried to show Lance how much he liked him—more than as just a FWB. And he'd tried to let Lance set the pace with sex. Yet Lance didn't seem to appreciate his efforts.

"We're dating," Sergio answered at last. "Aren't we? If we were friends with benefits, we would've had sex by now, not just fooled around."

Lance felt his anxiety cooling a little as Sergio continued: "I *like* you, man. I like hearing your voice—and those songs you sing. I like hanging out with you and looking at your face and your sexy freckles. I like your FIERCE smell. I like *you*. A lot."

"Well," Lance said, wanting to believe him, "I like you a lot too." It marked his first time post-Darrell to say that to a guy. In the months since their breakup he'd begun to wonder if he'd ever again find a guy to say it to.

"Great," Sergio exclaimed. "Then we're in sync!"

"So, um, when are we going out again?" Lance asked, suddenly eager to see him again.

"I can't tonight," Sergio said. "How about tomorrow?"

"Sounds good," Lance said. He was curious why Sergio couldn't go out tonight, but he didn't want to come off as too clingy and possessive, so he didn't ask.

After hanging up, he phoned Allie. Although he'd felt reluctant to tell Sergio what Allie had said, he didn't hesitate to tell her what Sergio had told him. "He said Kimiko said she thinks you're out of her league, plus you're still half-involved with Chip, and she's never dated anyone, so she's scared."

"Well, I don't think she's out of my league," Allie replied, while making her bed. "But as far as Chip goes, I can see her point. If I were her, I'd probably feel the same way."

"But Sergio says," Lance continued, "that she thinks there's too much mojo between you and her to just be friends."

"She said that?" Allie asked. "What else did she say?"

"That's it, I think. Then they had a fight because Sergio said maybe you two should be friends with benefits, and Kimiko didn't like him saying that."

"Friends with benefits?" Allie asked. That idea had never crossed her mind, and it didn't really appeal to her. "No, thanks."

"Yeah," Lance agreed. "I didn't think so either."

"So, are you and Sergio going out tonight?" Allie asked.

"No, he said he couldn't—although he didn't say why. I don't know why he didn't say why. I'm trying not to think about it. Do you want to hang out?"

"Yeah," Allie said. "I'd like that."

Lance drove over to her house and they ended up spending the entire day together, listening to music, surfing the Internet, talking about Kimiko and Sergio . . . Lance realized he was obsessing about him, and he had to resist the urge to text or IM him.

After dinner at Allie's, they went to the mall so he could get a new pair of swim goggles.

"Do you think he's had friends with benefits?" Lance asked her, as they walked through the sporting goods store. "When we first went out he said he'd done hookups, and even though he said he wants to try a relationship, he won't talk about who else he's seeing. Maybe he's got friends with benefits and hasn't told me. I hate this! At least with Darrell I knew he was too closeted to risk seeing anyone else." Lance stopped and searched a rack of goggles while he continued talking to Allie. "If Sergio likes me as much as he says he does, I don't get why he won't just say he wants to be a couple. I mean I understand he got dumped and felt hurt, but still . . . How long am I supposed to wait for him to get over it? It feels the same as waiting for Darrell to come out. It sucks to be waiting, not knowing what's going to happen."

He tried on several pairs of goggles before finally settling on one.

"And he didn't say what he's doing tonight?" Allie asked as they wandered to the food court to hang out.

"No. And after getting shot down at the dance for wanting to know who else he's seeing, I didn't want to ask."

They walked a few paces farther when Allie suddenly stopped. "So, don't look now but I think you're about to find out what he's doing tonight."

Lance followed her gaze across the tables to where Sergio sat eating ice cream with a tan-skinned, dark-haired guy. Lance's stomach gave a lurch. Instinctively, he pulled Allie back behind a nearby column.

"Who is that?" she whispered, even though they were way too far for Sergio to hear them.

"I don't know," Lance whispered back. He leaned on the column to steady himself and peeked around the corner. Was the guy a date, or a hookup, or a friend with benefits?

"I don't get a date vibe from them," Allie said, peering over Lance's shoulder. "Maybe he's a relative. They look a lot alike."

That was true; they did look kind of alike.

"But if he's a relative, why didn't Sergio just say he was going to meet a relative?" Lance took a deep breath, trying to calm the sinking feeling in his stomach. "See? This totally sucks, not knowing." He sneaked another look at Sergio talking and laughing with the guy. "Come on," Lance told Allie. "Let's get out of here!"

"You don't want to say hi and find out who the guy is?" Allie asked.

"No. No, I want go home."

As they drove away from the mall, Lance stayed quiet. Alternating waves of anger and hurt washed over him while the image of Sergio with the guy persisted in his mind.

"Just ask him tomorrow who it was," Allie suggested, patting Lance's shoulder as he stared sullenly out the windshield.

He didn't reply to her. He had a hard time getting to sleep that night, his thoughts still fixed on Sergio and the guy.

The following morning on the drive to church, Allie didn't ask about Sergio. And Lance didn't ask about Kimiko. Instead, they both focused on the hymns they were scheduled to sing that day, rehearsing in the car.

After lunch with Allie and some choir friends, Lance returned home. He was changing out of his church clothes when his cell rang with the ring tone he'd set for Sergio. Lance stared at the phone screen, steeling himself to answer.

"Hi." He finally picked up.

"What up?" Sergio said. "How was choir?"

"Good," Lance told him. "How's it going with you?"

"It's going good." Sergio yawned. "I slept late. Now I was just playing with Elton so he won't complain. Otherwise he gets jealous like: Why the hell don't you ever play with me, you stinking *pendejo*?"

Lance laughed politely even though he didn't know what *"pendejo"* meant and he didn't really feel like laughing. He wanted to see if Sergio would tell him the truth about the guy at the mall: "So, um, what did you do last night?"

"Went to the mall," Sergio said. "How about you?"

"Um, went to the mall too." Lance felt a little silly for

drawing this out rather than simply asking: who was the guy?

"Really?" Sergio lifted Elton back into his cage. "Which mall?"

"The same one you went to," Lance replied.

"You saw me there?" Sergio asked. "Why didn't you say hi?"

"Because you were busy with someone."

"Yeah, that was my cousin. You should've said hi."

"Well"—Lance kicked his shoes off—"how was I supposed to know he wasn't a date, or a hookup, or a friend with benefits?"

Sergio heard the annoyance in his voice. "Hey, chill, man. You're overreacting."

"So how am I supposed to react," Lance said in a hard tone, "if you won't tell me if you're still seeing other people?" A surge of anger swelled in his chest, rising into his throat. "This sucks, you know that? How would *you* feel if *I* were dating other people?"

"Well, if that's what you want to do . . . ," Sergio said, growing equally aggravated.

"No, that's not what I want to do! And I don't want to be wondering who else you're going out with either. If you don't want to be a couple, then I don't want to go out anymore!"

Lance tried to calm down, a little shocked he'd exploded like that. Yet under his anger breathed a little relief.

Sergio turned silent, not sure how to respond to

Lance's outburst. He didn't want to lose Lance, but . . . "I told you, man, I'm not ready to be a couple."

"Then it's over," Lance said. It stunned him that he'd said it. Should he take it back? Maybe now Sergio would change his mind, say that he *did* want to be a couple, and agree not go out with anybody else.

But instead, Sergio told him, "You're acting like a kid."

Lance winced, doubting himself. *Is Sergio right? Am I acting like a kid?*

"No," Lance said, his resolve returning. "*You're* the one who's not willing to commit."

It felt good to stand up for himself, even if it meant losing Sergio.

Both of them became quiet, each listening to his own breath, neither willing to change his mind nor knowing what more to say.

"Hello?" Sergio said at last, wondering if Lance had hung up on him.

"Yeah?" Lance replied, hoping that Sergio would apologize for having called him a kid.

"I guess . . . ," Sergio said, ". . . good-bye, then."

"Um, bye," Lance replied, while his stomach slipped down to his toes—at least that's what it felt like. *Oh, crap,* he thought as the line clicked off. *Did I really just do that?*

After getting dumped by Darrell, he'd come to think of himself as the one who got broken up with, not the one who did the breaking up. Shouldn't it feel better to ditch someone than to get ditched? In this case it didn't.

Immediately, he phoned Allie.

"Wow," she replied when he told her what he'd said to Sergio. "You really said that?"

"Um, yeah." He now wished he hadn't said it. "I shouldn't have, should I?"

"I don't know," Allie said. "Do *you* think you should've?"

"I don't know either," Lance told her. "I've never dumped anybody before. Shouldn't it feel easier than getting dumped?"

"See?" Allie replied. "That's what I've been going through with Chip. Do you want to come over? I'm baby-sitting Josh but you can color with us till he takes a nap."

"I'm on my way," Lance told her. Even though he'd left her only an hour earlier, he quickly finished changing clothes and headed out the door.

What lips my lips have kissed, and where, and why . . . That title line of an Edna Saint Vincent Millay sonnet echoed through Kimiko's mind on Sunday as she sat on her bedroom carpet, trying to conjure up a new poem of her own. But words simply wouldn't come—only questions about Allie.

Why did she kiss me? They couldn't possibly have any future together other than as friends. They were too different.

Kimiko put her pen down and gazed at herself in the mirror: She looked so plain. She felt so uncertain. She was so inexperienced. . . . Then she thought about Allie: beautiful, mature, cool, confident. . . .

So, why the heck did she kiss me? Just to test what it felt like to kiss a girl? Doesn't she realize how much it hurts to be toyed with like that? Has she no clue how much I like her?

A line from a Walt Whitman poem drifted into her thoughts: *Sometimes with one I love I fill myself with rage for fear I effuse unreturn'd love. . . .*

Do I love her? Kimiko wondered. *What would be the point? It can't go anywhere.* Even if Allie were truly bi, that didn't mean she'd want to date or be anything more than friends. And Kimiko definitely didn't want to be friends with benefits. It would be too frustrating to try to keep her feelings in check.

She got up from the carpet, walked to her bookshelf, and pulled out her copy of Whitman's *Leaves of Grass*. Turning to the section titled "Calamus," she read:

> But now I think there is no unreturn'd love—
> the pay is certain, one way or another;
> (I loved a certain person ardently, and my love
> was not return'd;
> Yet out of that, I have written these songs.)

Should I let myself love her, Kimiko wondered, *just to be a better poet?* But what if the experience didn't make her a better poet? What if all it did was break her heart and ruin their friendship?

A footnote at the bottom of the page included a different version of the last stanza:

> Doubtless I could not have perceived the universe, or written one of my poems, if I had not freely given myself to comrades, to love.

"Miko!" her mom called. "It's time for dinner."

Should I give myself freely to love? Kimiko wondered. *Should I give myself freely to Allie? Is that what she wants? But what if things don't work out? And what about my family?*

She closed the book and set it down on her desk. As

she headed downstairs, her cell rang: Sergio calling. She hit SILENCE and let the call roll to voice mail. Her anger at him had left, but she still felt confused about Allie. It worried her that he might confuse her even more. Better to wait till tomorrow.

When Kimiko got on the school bus the next morning and took her usual seat beside Sergio, she noticed right away his face scrunched with worry.

"'Sup?" she said.

"Do you forgive me?" He pressed his hands together, prayer-like.

"Yeah, you know I always do." Was that what his worry was about?

"Thanks," he said humbly. "How are you doing? Any news with Allie?"

"No." Kimiko shook her head and didn't say any more about it.

He decided not to pursue it either, afraid he might say something she'd get mad at again. Instead, he announced: "I got dumped again."

"What?" She gasped. "What happened?" She felt bad that she hadn't answered his calls. She tried to now make up for it by listening attentively while he told her about his call with Lance. "Wow . . . Sorry, dude."

"Why are guys so jealous and possessive?" he asked her as they reached school.

"Do you think you're more so than girls?" she replied, following him off the bus.

"Maybe not." He thought for a moment about his

experiences with Zelda and other girls. "I'm just not ready to be a couple. Why can't he accept that?"

"It sounds like you guys are in different places," Kimiko said philosophically. It felt a lot easier to talk about somebody else's relationship rather than her own. "He's ready for couple-hood and you're not. One of you has to change or it won't work."

Sergio thought about that as they walked toward their lockers. "And what about you and Allie? What are you guys going to do?"

"What can we do?" Kimiko answered. "We can't go back to just being friends. That would be too hard. And we can't be more than friends either. We can't be anything."

"Why not?" Sergio asked, at risk of her getting mad at him again. "You guys like each other so much. Just say for a moment that she wasn't still half-involved with that guy and you accepted that maybe she's not out of your league. If anything were possible, would you want to date her?"

"Dude . . ." Kimiko turned her combination lock and tried to stay calm. "That's not reality. You're forgetting my family. I've got to think about them, too. I can't just think about myself. That's selfish."

"What's your family got to do with it?" Sergio argued, opening his own locker and getting the books he needed. "It's *your* life."

"It's not only my life," Kimiko retorted. "What I do affects them, too. I don't want to hurt them."

"Doesn't that work the other way around, too?" Sergio continued while closing his locker. "Whatever they do affects you. Aren't they hurting you by not accepting you? I don't get why it's selfish to be honest about who you are. Doesn't it work both ways? Or are you and Dragon Lady going to play the Pretend Game all your life?"

Kimiko shut her locker and frowned at him. She already had enough to deal with; she didn't want to think about coming out to her family.

After school, she picked up her brother and drove to their karate classes. For the next hour she focused her attention solely on what transpired on the mat—kicking and punching at her opponents, concentrating on each and every movement. She forgot about Sergio, Allie, her family, and everything else going on. After class and a shower, she felt both exhausted and newly energized.

"How was karate?" her dad asked during dinner. He'd encouraged her from the time she'd first started, even when her mom had protested, "It's not for girls."

"It was good," Kimiko now answered and served herself some sliced beef.

"It was boring," her brother complained. He'd never liked karate. "I don't want to go anymore."

"It's good for you," their dad said from across the table.

"It gives me a headache," Yukio grumbled in between mouthfuls.

"Well, you have to do some exercise," their mom replied.

"Don't you want to be as good as your sister?" their dad asked.

"No," Yukio said.

Kimiko felt kind of bad for him. "If he doesn't like it," she told her parents, "why don't you let him do some other exercise?"

"Like what?" her mom asked.

Kimiko peered at her brother. "What other exercise would you like to do?"

Yukio thought for a moment. "Nothing. I don't like exercise."

"See?" Their mom gave a shrug. "If he didn't do karate, he wouldn't do anything except sit and eat and play games. Maybe *you* should do some other exercise," she told Kimiko. "Something more attractive for a girl."

Kimiko's skin prickled and she recalled her conversation with Sergio. "I don't care if it's attractive or not."

"Well, you should care," her mom insisted.

"Why should I?" Kimiko erupted. "Just to please you? Why can't you just let me be me?"

Her mom narrowed her eyes at her. "I don't let you be you? I don't let you dress however you want and do whatever you want?"

"No, you don't!" The words exploded from Kimiko as from a long-dormant volcano. "You've never accepted me. You only pretend to. You want me to be something I'm not. Why can't you just accept me?"

"Miko, I do accept you. I only want for you to be a normal girl—is that too much to ask a daughter?"

"I don't want to be normal!" Kimiko felt herself losing control. "I've never been normal—not what you consider normal—and I never will be." That was the closest she'd ever come to admitting she was a lesbian. "And you know it! Why don't you just stop pretending?"

She realized she was asking herself the question as much as her mom, and suddenly the words sprang from her mouth: "I'm a lesbian. I always have been and always will be."

A blanket of silence descended upon the room. Her brother peered blankly at her. Her dad set his silverware down. Her mom shook her head angrily while glancing at her husband, then at their son, then back to their daughter.

"Go to your room!" she ordered Kimiko, her voice quavering.

"Not until you accept it." Kimiko swallowed hard to quench the dryness in her throat.

Her mom's face turned redder as she shifted her gaze. "Yukio, go up to your room!"

"I haven't finished eating," he protested, quickly digging his spoon into his rice.

"You've eaten enough." Their mom reached across the table and pulled his plate away. "Now, do what I tell you!"

Yukio glanced at their dad, who nodded for him to obey. Yukio shuffled out of the room while glancing over his shoulder, not wanting to leave.

"You're a selfish daughter," her mom told Kimiko and began to clear the dishes. "You think only about what you want!"

Kimiko cringed, but then regained her resolve. "No, Mom, *you're* selfish—by trying to make me into what *you* want."

Her mom flinched, her eyes turning shiny with anger and tears. The plates she held abruptly clattered onto the table. Kimiko stood to help but her mom waved her away. "Leave me alone!"

"It's okay," Kimiko's dad said, gesturing for Kimiko to sit down.

"It's not okay," her mom countered, restacking the dishes and carrying them from the room. Inside the kitchen, the plates rattled onto the counter and the sink water began to run, along with what sounded like muffled sobs.

Kimiko guiltily hung her head. She wished she could put her cap on and pull it down over her. She felt her dad studying her and waited for him to say something about her announcement. Would he be as angry as her mom?

His voice came out level, stern. "You've upset your mother."

"I'm sorry," Kimiko said. "I just can't pretend anymore."

Her dad was silent for what seemed like a century until at last he said, "I understand."

She glanced up eagerly. Did that mean he accepted her? Although he didn't come out and say that, his face softened. And he gave what seemed to be a subtle nod of approval. Her family had never been one to make expressive shows of emotion. This might be the closest she'd ever get to a declaration of acceptance.

"I love you, Dad." She wanted to do something to show how much she loved him. Without him, she'd be lost. She stood and wrapped her arms around him.

He patted her wrist in return. "You're our daughter."

"Thanks," she said, breathing in his talcum and tobacco smell. A reassuring smell.

From the kitchen came the sound of her mom clanging pots and rattling dishes. Kimiko began to gather the remaining plates. It was her responsibility to help clear the table, and she didn't want her mom to become even angrier.

But her dad told her to leave them. "It's better to let me talk with her."

Kimiko nodded. She grabbed her cap from the back of her chair and headed upstairs to her room. She closed the door, sat down on her bed, and tried to absorb what she'd done. It felt huge, like *everything* had suddenly changed—her whole entire life. She took out her phone and called Sergio.

"I did it," she whispered at first and then, unable to control herself, shouted, "I did it!"

"With who?" he kidded her, but she ignored it.

"I came out to them at dinner," Kimiko explained, and told him what had happened. "I think my dad's okay with it. But my mom . . . She'll probably sulk for days. The same as she always does."

"Ding-dong, the witch is dead," Sergio began to sing, *"the witch is dead—"*

"Shush, dude. It's not funny."

"Don't let her get to you," Sergio replied. "You did a hella thing."

"Yeah, tell her that."

"Okay, put her on!"

Just as he said that, a knock sounded at the door, nearly sending Kimiko out of her skin.

"Shit! Call you back."

She shuffled to the door, bracing to face her mom. Instead, she opened it to find her brother.

"What?" Kimiko asked, sighing with relief.

He looked up at her, his mouth hanging down with confusion. "What's a lesbian?"

She grabbed his arm and yanked him into her room, closing the door again.

"It's a gay woman," she explained in a low voice.

"Oh." He glanced down at the carpet, thinking. Then he looked up again. "What do you mean by gay?"

Even though he might not know the word *lesbian*, he'd surely heard the word *gay* at school. But obviously, nobody had ever discussed with him what it actually meant. Kimiko fidgeted with her cap, trying to think of how to explain it without getting graphic on him, how to put it in a way his eight-year-old brain could understand.

"It means . . . I'm attracted to other girls . . . and one day I want to fall in love with a woman, and get married to her instead of a man, and have a family with her."

Yukio watched her face as if waiting for more. "That's it?"

"Yeah, basically."

He wiped his nose and glanced around her room. "Do you have anything to eat? I'm still hungry."

His response surprised her only for an instant. She rummaged around her dresser and finally found an Almond Joy left over from Halloween in the bottom of her backpack.

Happy with that, he returned to his room. She laid down on her bed, and as she thought about what she'd explained to him, thoughts of Allie floated back to her mind.

FIFTEEN

"Do you think I did the right thing to break up with him?" Lance asked Allie when they went to get haircuts together later that week.

"Are you having second thoughts?" she asked.

"Um, no . . . Yes . . . Maybe . . ." Lance had been thinking and rethinking about Sergio ever since their breakup. "I mean, I really like him. And I tried to go along . . . accepting that he's bi . . . fooling around with him. . . . I'm just not willing to go any further without him committing to being a couple."

"It sounds like you did what you needed to do," Allie consoled him.

"Yeah? So, what now?" he asked.

"I guess you let go of him and move on," she replied.

Lance thought about that. "Do you think maybe he'll change his mind?"

"Who knows? But you shouldn't wait around for it."

He knew she was right. Nonetheless, when he got home he immediately went online to see if there might be a message from Sergio. But nope: no e-mail, no IM.

Frustrated, he slumped down in his chair.

The following days dragged by, while brokenhearted show tunes invaded his head. One moment it was "Losing My Mind" from *Follies*. . . . The next it was *South Pacific*'s "I'm Gonna Wash That Man Right Outta My Hair."

During lunch at school one day, he watched Darrell sitting with Fiona, chatting and laughing, looking genuinely happy together. Could Sergio have been right? Maybe Darrell truly was bi.

Lance turned to Allie. "Do you think I should apologize to Darrell?"

"Huh?" She followed Lance's gaze across the cafeteria. "Apologize for what?"

Lance gave a shrug. "Maybe I shouldn't have pushed him to come out."

"I think you need to stop blaming yourself every time you break up," Allie said. Then she paused and thought for a moment. "Even though I'm feeling the same way about Chip."

Lance let out a sigh. "Maybe I should've just accepted him. Darrell, I mean."

"Well, if it'll make you feel better," Allie encouraged him, "go ahead: Tell him you're sorry. Then *move on*!"

"Yeah, I know, right?"

Although Lance wasn't convinced he needed to apologize, a couple of days later he was walking down the hallway where Darrell had his locker—and there he was. Lance realized this was his chance.

"Um, hi," he said. It was the first time he'd spoken to Darrell since their final phone call.

"Hi." Darrell's gaze darted around the hall, as though checking who might see them together.

"Um . . ." Lance mumbled and gathered his thoughts. "I just want to tell you that I'm sorry."

Darrell's face creased. "Sorry for what?"

Lance shrugged, feeling a little foolish. "Sorry that I didn't accept you and that I judged you and tried to push you to come out."

Darrell glanced over his shoulder again to make sure nobody was listening.

"I don't want there to be any bad blood between us," Lance continued and extended his hand. "So I want to say good luck to you and Fiona."

Darrell stared at Lance's hand, looking sort of mystified, and hastily shook it. "Thanks. I've got to go."

"All right, thanks," Lance said and watched him walk away. Even though it had felt weird and awkward to apologize, he was glad he'd done it.

"Feel better?" Allie asked after school when he told her about it.

"Yeah," he said.

"So are you going to apologize to Sergio, too?"

"What for?"

"I don't know. Just asking."

The question prompted him to think about the idea. He didn't feel like he had anything to apologize for. Nevertheless, when he got home he looked up Sergio's friend page again, wishing things had turned out differently. From atop the computer monitor, the plush Irish setter that Sergio had given him peered down over the screen, its big brown eyes just like Sergio's.

Lance stood up from the desk, grabbed the pup, and flopped down onto the bed with it. Then he closed his eyes for a nap, hoping to take his mind off of Sergio.

On Saturday morning, Sergio woke up with Lance's teddy bear staring him squarely in the face. Sergio reached groggily across the pillow and pushed the little bear away. Then he pulled the pillow over his face to block the morning light and tried to go back to sleep . . . but thoughts of Lance kept intruding. He never should've gone out with him. He'd known he was going to get dumped. Why had he let himself get involved?

Unable to stop thinking, he threw the covers off, slammed his feet to the floor, and grabbed the bear by one ear. Then he swung open the closet, threw the stupid thing into the black hole of junk, and banged the door shut. But that didn't really make him feel any better.

"Morning," he grumbled to his parents when he went to breakfast. While his dad read the Spanish newspaper across the table, his mom made scrambled eggs and *chorizo* for Sergio.

"Careful, it's hot," she said, setting the steaming plate in front of him.

"Thanks," he mumbled.

"Is something wrong, *mijo*?" She often used the

Spanish words for "my son" when she was worried about him. "You seem upset," she said, sitting down beside him.

He chewed his eggs, debating what to tell her. "Lance dumped me."

Sergio's dad glanced up, suddenly interested. He gave Sergio's mom a hopeful smile and then turned to him. "So, what about the girl you were seeing?"

"Serena," his mom chimed in.

"I told you"—Sergio set his fork down—"I'm not interested in her. Look, I know you'd rather I go out with a girl, but I'm going to go out with who *I* want, not who *you* want."

He waited for his parents to respond. His dad gave a disappointed grunt and returned to his paper. His mom let out a long, wistful sigh. After finishing his eggs and sausage, Sergio rinsed his plate, shoved it into the dishwasher, and returned to his room.

When Kimiko came over that afternoon, he griped to her about the conversation. "I wish I was still going out with Lance just to make my point."

"Are you going to call him?" she asked.

"He dumped me, remember?" Sergio lifted Elton out of his cage and began to play with him on the carpet while Kimiko put on some music.

"But he dumped you," she reminded Sergio, "because you didn't want to be a couple. I bet he'd take you back if you changed your mind."

Sergio thought about that for a moment. "He probably would've dumped me anyway. I knew he was going to."

"You know the other day in history class," Kimiko countered, "we talked about a 'self-fulfilling prophecy.' That's when you believe something is going to happen, and so you end up making it happen. It made me think about you and Lance."

"Huh?" Sergio asked as she plopped down onto the carpet beside him. "Why?"

"Because you were so worried about being dumped, you set it up so Lance would dump you."

"Thanks, Freud-ette. How much do I owe you?"

"Dude," Kimiko insisted, "you need to get over your fear of being dumped. Lance isn't Zelda."

"Maybe I'll just stick with Elton," Sergio said, picking him up and nuzzling him. "You'll never dump me, will you, boy?"

Elton sniffed him as if actually understanding. Then he responded by pooping out three hard little brown turds.

Kimiko giggled uproariously and grabbed a tissue to pick up the mess. Sergio didn't find it quite so funny.

CHAPTER SIXTEEN

A little before midnight Saturday, Kimiko returned home. Her mom and dad were waiting up as usual, watching TV.

"I'm home," Kimiko said.

In the past, her mom would've asked if Kimiko had eaten dinner and prepared her a bedtime snack. Tonight her mom wordlessly stood up from the TV, padded upstairs to her room, and closed the door.

"How much longer is she going to be this way?" Kimiko asked her dad.

"Give her time," he replied.

Ever since Kimiko had come out, her mom had barely even acknowledged her, no longer correcting how Kimiko sat or harping about her short hair. At the dinner table, she pretended as if Kimiko weren't even there.

At first Kimiko had told herself she didn't care. It was a relief to no longer be constantly criticized, and she figured her mom would get over brooding after a few days, as she always had in the past. But as the days became a week and the sulking continued, Kimiko began to worry: Would it ever end?

"It's making me crazy," she told Sergio and Serena during lunch one day.

"She probably needs time to adjust," Serena said.

"Adjust to what?" Kimiko swirled her french fry in ketchup. "I'm the same person I was before. . . . I should've just kept my mouth shut."

"You are getting crazy!" Sergio said. "Are you forgetting how miserable you were in the closet?"

"I'm still miserable," Kimiko said.

"Because of your mom?" Sergio asked and grinned slyly. "Or because of Allie?"

Kimiko scowled across the table at him. Coming out had temporarily taken her mind off of Allie. But now that the initial excitement had settled down, she found herself once more thinking about Allie and wondering: Was Allie thinking of her?

Since the last time she'd been with Kimiko, Allie had picked up the phone to call her nearly a million times. She thought about her every day, trying to sort out how she felt, debating what to do, wondering what their kiss meant. So many questions swirled around her mind.

Did the kiss prove she was bi? Or gay? Or straight but curious? What was she? *Who* was she? And what did it mean in terms of Kimiko?

Even though they'd agreed to just be friends, did she want to try to pursue Kimiko as more than a friend? And what should she do about Chip? She wanted to come to some sort of resolution about their relationship.

Should she let him know she thought she might be bi? Given his reaction to the *Girl Panic* manga and her sex dream, he probably wouldn't be hugely surprised. But what if he told other people at school? She wasn't ready for that. What she really wanted was to tell him that their relationship was over—but she knew he wouldn't want to break up.

And how would their breakup affect their group? Although it wouldn't change anything with Lance, it might be awkward with everybody else. Nevertheless, she had to do something.

"Can I talk to you after school?" she asked Chip at the end of lunch one day.

"Huh? Sure." He grinned from ear to ear as if hoping she were going to say their break was over and she wanted to get back together.

"Can you wait for me while I talk to him?" she asked Lance.

"Of course," he replied. "Good luck with it."

When she arrived at her locker after last period, Chip was already there waiting for her.

"Want to go talk in my car?" he asked and insisted on carrying her backpack. Everything he did—opening the car door for her, flipping down the visor for shade—made her feel guiltier than ever. Why did he have to be so nice?

"I've missed you," he said from across the car. "Even though we see each other every day, it hasn't been the same."

"I'm sorry," she said and tried to organize her thoughts.

"That's okay." He rested a hand on her shoulder. "So, what's going on?"

"I thought we should talk," she said. "About us . . . About me."

"Okay." He nodded for her to go on.

She took a breath. "I think maybe . . ." she shifted uncomfortably in her seat, ". . . I'm bisexual."

His face showed no surprise. "Yeah, I figured that . . . since—you know—stuff you said. . . . It's cool." He ran his fingertips through her curls. "I can work with that. We can still be together."

What did he mean? She recalled Kimiko telling her about Edna Saint Vincent Millay and her husband. "You mean like an open relationship?"

"Yeah." He nodded, expressionless. "If that's what you want."

"No, I don't want that." She pulled her head away from his hand. "Besides, I'm not sure yet that I am bi. I need to explore first if that's really who I am. I'm not ready to tell other people or anything. I only wanted to tell you."

"Well . . ." He kept his eyes on her. "Like I said before: I'll wait for you . . . till you decide."

The pain she heard in his voice made her stomach hurt.

"No," she insisted. "That's not fair to you. I don't want you to wait for me. I think you should explore other options."

"I don't want to explore other options." He gave

his head a forceful shake. His eyes made it clear that he needed and wanted her. "I love you."

"Look, I'm sorry. I really am." She gently took hold of his hand. "But it's just not going to work out between us."

His face didn't register that he understood, until slowly his eyes began to brim with tears. She wanted to cry too. But that would only make the breakup harder.

"I'm really sorry," she repeated and gave his hand a squeeze. Before he could say anything else, she opened the door and climbed from the car. While crossing the parking lot she texted Lance: *Where r u?*

He replied right away and she met him at his car. The instant she closed the door behind her, she erupted into tears.

"I feel so sad." She sobbed and wiped her eyes with a tissue. "But it's a relief, too." As Lance drove her home, he listened while she cried. And when they got to her house, he went inside, staying with her until her tears subsided. "At least I feel free now," she told him.

"You mean as in free to call Kimiko?" Lance asked, patting her shoulder.

That wasn't exactly what she'd meant, but it was part of it. Later that evening, alone in her room, she pulled out her phone.

Kimiko was in the middle of dinner when her cell vibrated in her jeans pocket. Upon sliding it out and seeing Allie's name, Kimiko's heart began to race like crazy. She wanted to answer, but her family had a rule of no dinnertime calls.

She didn't want to give her mom any cause for more anger.

During the rest of the meal, she could barely eat, thinking only of Allie. What should she say when they talked? Would Allie mention the kiss? As soon as Kimiko finished clearing the table, she raced upstairs to her bedroom and listened to the voice mail.

"Hi, Kimiko. It's Allie." Her voice sounded a little shaky and nervous. "I'm just calling to say hi and see how you're doing. Give me a call sometime. I hope you're okay . . . I miss you."

Kimiko had missed her, too. Even though she'd told herself they couldn't be friends or girlfriends or anything, she couldn't stop thinking about her. She now played the message over and over, listening to Allie's voice. In order to calm down, she shook out her arms and kicked her legs, until her breath finally slowed enough to phone her.

"'Sup, dude?"

"Hi!" Allie said. She'd just finished helping her mom put Josh to bed. "It's great to hear your voice. How're you doing?"

"Pretty good." Kimiko somehow managed to steady her voice. "I came out to my family."

"That's awesome!" Allie exclaimed, closing her bedroom door. "Congrats!"

"Thanks." Kimiko nervously swung the bill of her cap from one side to the other. "Except my mom stopped talking to me."

"Oh, gosh," Allie said, sitting down on her loveseat. "I'm sorry to hear that."

"It's okay. So, what's new with you?"

"Well . . . I guess my big news is I broke up with Chip."

Kimiko remained quiet, absorbing the implication: Allie was now availably single.

"Hello?" Allie said. "You still there?"

"Yeah, yeah, I'm here," Kimiko said. "So . . . are you okay with the breakup?"

"Yeah. It felt like we had already broken up. He's a great guy but it was over. So . . . I had a good cry with Lance."

"That's good," Kimiko replied, uncertain what else to say.

"So, like, how is the math going?" Allie asked, not wanting to dwell on her breakup.

"It's going better," Kimiko answered. "Thanks to you."

"I'd be happy to help you again sometime," Allie offered. She hoped she wasn't pushing things, but she felt so excited to talk with Kimiko again. "If you need any help, I mean. Or if you'd like to just hang out, I'd like that, too."

"So would I," Kimiko said, her voice a little wobbly. She wished she'd never told Allie that they should *just* be friends. She wished they could be more than that. At least Allie was single now. But *could* they be more than friends? "Would you like to hang out this weekend?" Kimiko asked.

"That would be super," Allie replied.

The conversation flowed a little more easily after that even though Kimiko could barely control her excitement.

She told Allie more about coming out to her family; Allie told her more about her breakup with Chip; they talked about their brothers, and school, and karate, and church choir. As soon as they hung up, Kimiko phoned Sergio.

"Dude, she called! We're going to hang out this weekend." She pre-empted any of his wiseass comments by adding: *"As friends."*

"Riiight," he replied. "And we know how well that worked last time."

"Oh, shush!" she told him.

"So, did she mention how devastated Lance was about dumping me?" Sergio asked.

"Oh, yeah," Kimiko joked. "I forgot to mention that."

"Really? She *did*?"

"No, dude. She didn't mention him."

"Oh," Sergio said.

"But if she had," Kimiko said, hearing the sadness in his voice, "I'm sure she would've said he's devastated and wants to get back together."

"Thanks," Sergio said. Even though he knew she was making it up, he hoped that maybe it was true.

SEVENTEEN

After hearing about Kimiko's talk with Allie, Sergio stared at his phone, missing Lance even more than before. He moped around his bedroom, worked out on his bench press to distract himself, and then binged on chocolates till he overdosed.

Maybe I should call him, Sergio thought. *But do I really want to be a couple? And would he be willing to take me back?*

Later that night, his mom tapped on his door and asked to speak to him. She sat down in his desk chair while he took a seat on the bed.

"I talked to Padre Ralph today," she said.

He was their nice but stodgy old parish priest who walked with a waddle and whistled to himself. Sergio's mom sometimes sought him out to talk about her problems and ask his advice.

"Yeah, so?" Sergio asked her. He already sensed what was coming.

"I talked to him about you," his mom continued, and he knew she meant about his bisexuality. "He says you need to pray to change."

"Change into what?" Sergio crossed his arms. "I don't want to change. I'm happy with who I am."

"You don't seem happy," she replied.

"That's *not* because I'm bi," he argued. "I felt like crap when Zelda dumped me too."

His mom was quiet a moment, her eyes fixed on the crucifix she'd hung on the wall above his headboard. She'd put a cross up over every bed in the house. "Padre Ralph said that as long as you don't act on it, it's not a sin."

"Too late, Mom. I've already acted on it."

Her mouth drooped into a brooding look.

"Look, Mom, I'm not going to change, okay? I like who I am, even if you don't."

At that, she winced a little. "Of course I like you. You're my son. I love you."

"Well, if you can love me," Sergio countered, "don't you think that God—who supposedly *is* love—can love me too?"

A tiny smile appeared on her worried face. "I want you to be happy, *mijo*."

"That's what I want too," Sergio said. "And the only way I can do that is by being me—even if sometimes it sucks."

"What about your friend?" she asked, and Sergio knew she meant Lance. "He seems like a nice boy."

"He is." Sergio smiled, glad she liked him.

"Then why did you two fight?" She sounded concerned, maybe even worried.

"We didn't really fight. It's just . . . he wants to be a couple and I don't."

"Why don't you?" she asked, and her question kind of annoyed him.

"You mean besides the fact you don't want me to date a guy?"

She folded her hands on her lap, looking kind of contrite.

"I guess," Sergio continued, "because—"

He stopped short, suddenly unsure. Why didn't he want to be a couple? Because Lance might dump him? Well, he'd dumped Sergio anyway. It seemed like what Kimiko had said: a self-fulfilling prophecy.

"I guess I wasn't ready," he told his mom.

She nodded understandingly. "I'm afraid you're going to make your life harder for yourself."

"I think I already have," he admitted.

Her face creased once more with worry. "Is there anything I can do?"

"No," he mumbled, unable to think of anything. Maybe he just needed to stop being afraid.

"*Te quiero, mijo.*" She stood, wrapped her arms around him, and gave him a fierce embrace. "I love you."

"I love you, too," he replied. At least *she* hadn't dumped him.

"So, do you think I should call him?" Sergio asked Kimiko the following day while they bought guinea pig food at the pet store. He'd related during lunch his conversation with his mom about Lance.

"Are you ready to be a couple?" Kimiko asked.

"I think so," Sergio replied. "The entire universe appears to be conspiring for it. . . . And I'm not dating anybody else anyway . . . But most of all, I miss him. A whole lot."

"Then it sounds like you're ready," Kimiko said as they went to the cash register.

"But what if he's not interested?" Sergio asked while they drove to his house. "That would be like getting dumped twice."

"Well," she argued, "at least you won't wonder the rest of your life if you could've gotten back together."

Sergio pondered that as they arrived home.

"What do you think I should do, Elton?" Sergio asked after feeding him. He answered himself in a high-pitched voice, "Call him, you stupid *pendejo*! What the hell is the matter with you? You want me to poop on you again?"

"See?" Kimiko giggled. "You'd better do what he says!"

"Okay, okay. I'll call. But you can't listen." He whisked his hand for her to leave the room. But as she started to go, he changed his mind, afraid he'd lose his resolve. "Wait! Don't go till he answers! I'll give you the signal, okay?" He took a deep breath, lifted his cell, and dialed. . . .

Lance was in the family room asking his dad a question for chemistry homework when *South Pacific*'s "Some Enchanted Evening," abruptly began to play in his pocket. It was Sergio's ring tone.

Lance pulled out the phone and stared at the screen, feeling both thrilled and startled. Had Sergio changed his mind?

"Um . . . would you mind if I answer?" he asked his dad.

"Go ahead." His dad gave him a goofy smile.

"Thanks," Lance said. He bolted upstairs to his room as he answered the phone. "Um, hello?"

"What up?" Sergio said, his voice quivering a little. He signaled Kimiko and she stepped out of the room, closing the door behind her.

"I was just talking with my dad," Lance said, letting Rufus into the bedroom before closing his door. "What are you up to?"

"Nothing." Sergio nervously slid down to the carpet beside his bed. "Kimiko came over . . . And . . . Now I'm calling you. . . . I guess you already know that. . . ." He banged the phone against his forehead, certain he was sounding like a doofus. "So . . . like . . . how have you been?"

"Um, okay . . ." Lance sat down on his bed and Rufus climbed up beside him. "Good, I guess. And you?"

"Good too, I guess."

"Um, that's good," Lance said, both relieved and excited to be talking with him.

Sergio leaned back against his bed and scanned his room, trying to decide what else to say. ". . . And kind of sad," he admitted, "because of . . . you know . . . I miss you, man."

Lance heard the sadness in his voice and felt his own gloominess. "I miss you, too."

"You do?" Sergio's pulse sped up; maybe Lance *wouldn't* dump him a second time.

"Um, yeah, I do."

Sergio sat up straighter, working up his nerve for what he wanted to say.

"So . . . I've been kind of thinking . . . about the stuff we talked about . . . you know . . . about being a couple?"

"You have?" Lance replied, his heart beating faster.

"Yeah." Sergio swallowed the knot in his throat. "I've been thinking maybe we could try it . . . and see if we can make it work together. . . . That's if you still want to."

Lance thought for a moment, wondering if Sergio really meant it. "Is that what *you* want?"

"Yeah." Sergio's legs jiggled anxiously. "If that's what you want, then that's what I want."

"But what about whoever else you're seeing?" Lance asked, curious as to what had changed.

"I'm not seeing anybody else," Sergio replied.

Then why were you so opposed to being a couple before? Lance wondered. And to be sure, he asked, "No friends with benefits or anything?"

"No, man. No one."

Lance tried to keep a grip on the excitement building inside him. "So, are you sure you want to do this?"

"Yeah," Sergio said. "Nervous . . . but . . . I'm sure if you're sure."

"Well, I'm nervous too," Lance admitted. "But I'm sure."

"You are?" Sergio hadn't expected this to go so smoothly. "You seem so determined."

"Yeah," Lance agreed. "Because I like you."

"I like you, too," Sergio said, sliding back against his bed. "I've missed you a lot."

"So, um, when can we go out again?" Lance asked, letting go of all his restraint.

Sergio wished they could go out tonight—like *right now*, even if it was a school night. But it was kind of late and he still had homework to do and he didn't want to seem totally gaga. Instead they agreed to get together on Saturday. It was only a day away anyway.

They stayed talking for a while more. Sergio told Lance about the conversation with his mom about Padre Ralph. And Lance told Sergio about the school musical, *Man of La Mancha*, which he was going to audition for.

When they finally hung up, Sergio sat quietly for a moment, basking in the glow he felt. Then he leaped up and did a happy dance across the room to the door.

"Hey, where did you go?" he called out to Kimiko. He jogged to the living room and found her watching a soccer game with his dad.

"We're going out again!" he announced, jumping onto the sofa beside her.

"Sweet!" She high-fived him.

Then he glanced over at his dad, who turned from the TV and forced a faint smile. It wasn't exactly the seal of approval, but it was something, and Sergio took it gladly.

EIGHTEEN

"Guess who called?" Lance phoned to tell Allie as soon as he'd hung up with Sergio.

"Woo-hoo!" she exclaimed, immediately guessing he meant Sergio. "So what happened? What did I miss? Who said what to who? Tell me! Tell me!"

"He wants to try being a couple!" Lance explained while petting and playing with Rufus, unable to sit still.

"Super!" Allie cheered again, leaning forward in her desk chair.

"He said he's not seeing anyone else," Lance continued. "Why didn't he just say that earlier?"

"Maybe he wasn't ready to commit," Allie answered. "He had to lose you to realize how much he wants you."

"Gee, that sounds good." Lance's cheeks were starting to hurt from smiling so widely. "He said he wants to try to make it work together."

"You can't get much better than that."

"So, we're going to get together Saturday. Isn't that when you're seeing Kimiko? Maybe we should double-date."

"Hmm, I'm not sure we're ready to call ours a date," Allie said. "We've still got a lot to sort out."

"Oh, yeah." Lance let out a long breath. "I guess I'm just excited—like I want to bounce around the room. I should probably take Rufus for a run. That's what I'll do." He grabbed his sneakers to tug them on. "Call you later, okay?"

"Sure. Have fun!" After hanging up, Allie went back to the math she'd been working on, and her thoughts returned to Kimiko. Even though she wasn't ready to call their meeting a date, she almost felt excited enough to bounce around the room, too. It probably would be a good idea for the four of them to hang out, at least for a little while, to help them all calm down.

On Saturday morning after Kimiko showered and dressed, she steeled herself to head downstairs, dreading her mom's silent treatment. Over a week had passed since she'd come out and her mom was still sulking.

"'Sup?" Kimiko said when she got to the kitchen.

"Good morning," her dad replied, looking up from the Japanese news on his laptop. "Sleep well?"

"All right," Kimiko said, preparing herself a bowl of cereal with soy milk. "Where's Mom?"

"In the garden." Her dad nodded toward the back-yard. "I spoke with her again last night." Clearly, he meant he'd spoken to her about Kimiko. "I told her she needs to talk with you. But you need to talk with her, too. You both need to talk."

"I've *tried* to talk with her," Kimiko protested, even though it had just been small talk: "'Sup?" and "Later." "She just ignores me."

"Well, try harder," her dad said. His tone was serious but his eyes were encouraging.

While Kimiko ate her cereal, she mulled over what he'd told her. Should she try to talk with her mom? Was it worth the risk of getting chewed out again?

Kimiko finished eating, rinsed her bowl in the sink, and peered out the window. Her mom was dragging one of her bucket-size potted plants across the brick patio. She paused to catch her breath, took off a garden glove, and wiped her brow. Kimiko placed her bowl in the dishwasher and glanced at her dad. He nodded as if reading her mind. Then she shuffled out the back door.

"Want some help?" she asked and made herself smile at her mom.

"No need." Her mom pulled her glove back on and grabbed the pot's rim.

Ignoring her mother's protest, Kimiko took hold of the other side of the clay. "Where do you want it?"

"Why can't you ever listen to me?" her mom snapped, letting go of the pot.

The rim slipped from Kimiko's hands. She leaped back, gasping. The heavy pot thudded onto the brick patio, and the clay cracked to pieces.

For a long silent moment, Kimiko and her mom stared down at the uprooted plant, the broken pot, the spilled earth. Kimiko had suspected that trying to talk with her wouldn't go well, and it had gone even worse than she'd feared.

"Why can't *you* listen to *me*?" she said softly.

Her mom gave her a sharp look, then bent down to sweep up the scattered earth with her gloved hands. "I *do* listen to you."

"No, you don't," Kimiko insisted, her voice breaking. "Ever since I was little, I've tried and tried to talk to you, but you never listen. You pretend like you do, but you never have." She paused to take a breath, struggling to keep her lip from trembling. "I always tried to be the best daughter I could be, but you never saw that. You could only see what you thought I should be." She brought a hand to her cheek and wiped her face. "I'm sorry—really, really sorry, Mom—that I'm not the girl you wanted. But I never will be."

She spun around to hide her tears—the tears she didn't want to be there—and hurried back across the patio. It had been years since she cried in front of her mom. She'd thought she was over that.

As she burst into the kitchen, her dad glanced up with concern. "What happened?"

"I tried, Dad. I really tried!" She crossed the room, too upset to explain anymore, bounded upstairs, and slammed her bedroom door.

Why do I let her get to me like that? Kimiko thought. *Why did I bother to even try to talk with her? I don't care if she never speaks to me again. Ever.*

She grabbed a tissue and blew her nose, while her

head burned from the argument. She tried to call Sergio, but his phone was turned off; he was probably still sleeping.

"I had a blow-out with my mom," she said into his voice mail. "Can you call me when you wake up? I really need to talk to you."

She hung up, tossed away her tissue, grabbed a new one, and checked her computer to see which of her friends was online. She couldn't find anyone.

Glancing down out of her window at the backyard patio, she watched her mom carefully prop the uprooted plant against a flower bed wall, sweep up the spilled earth, and pile together the pieces of broken clay.

"She cares more about her plants than about me," Kimiko muttered.

Her mom must have sensed her watching her and glanced up.

Kimiko quickly drew back from the window and grabbed her motorcycle jacket, eager to get out of the house. The previous night, Allie had phoned and proposed that they make their get together a foursome with Lance and Sergio, "to help us chill." Kimiko had jumped at the idea. She could use a little chill to cool her jitters. She'd called Sergio and brought him on board with the idea. But she wasn't supposed to meet them till later, and she had to go somewhere *now*. Or she'd implode.

While she checked herself in the mirror, she heard the muffled sounds that came from downstairs. Her mom opened and closed the back door, returning inside, and began to argue with her dad. Kimiko padded softly across the carpet, cracked her door open, and tried to make out what they were saying.

"Because she doesn't realize what she's doing," her mom argued. "She's making a foolish decision."

Kimiko cringed. *This is hopeless; she'll never understand.*

"If that's her nature," her dad said, "you can't change it."

"No, but she can change," her mom persisted.

"Maybe not," her dad said. "Maybe *you* need to change—or lose her."

Kimiko waited for a response, but her mom stayed quiet. Kimiko closed the door again and leaned against it, bracing herself to go downstairs. She didn't want to see her mom right now, but she didn't want to stay in her room, either. Could she sneak past them? Or just hurry out? She grabbed a new tissue, dabbed her nose once more, and swung the door open.

She leaped back, startled by the figure facing her. In the hallway stood her mom, looking equally surprised.

For a moment, the two simply stared through the doorway, each waiting for the other to make the next move.

"Can I come in?" her mom asked in a soft, resigned voice.

It took a minute before Kimiko could answer. "Yes."

She stepped back and her mom slowly walked in, neither smiling nor frowning. Showing no emotion, only self-control. Her "samurai face," Sergio called it.

Her mom smoothed the bedspread, sat down on the edge of the bed, and motioned to Kimiko with her head. "I'm here to listen."

Kimiko remained standing, responding with a look that said: *Are you sure?*

What should she say? Where should she start? Would her mom truly listen?

"I'm sorry," Kimiko said, trying to keep her voice steady. "I haven't turned out the way you wanted. I can't change who I—"

"But you're making life so difficult for yourself," her mom cut in.

"No, Mom," Kimiko said, a little amazed by her own calm. "*You're* the one making life difficult for me. Everybody else accepts me, even Dad. Why can't *you*?"

Her mom became quiet, pressed her fingertips against her eyes, and shook her head. "Ever since you were little, the entire time you were growing up, I kept asking myself, 'What am I doing wrong? Why is this happening?' This isn't what I wanted for your life."

Kimiko heard the sadness in her voice. She grabbed a tissue again, fearing she might need it. "What do you want for my life, Mom?"

"You know"—Her mom made a sweeping gesture with her hand—"what every mother wants for her daughter. For you to get married, raise children, work, be happy."

"That's what I want, too, Mom. Can't you understand?" She felt like she must not be speaking clearly. "I just want it with a woman, not a man."

Her mom cocked her head slightly, her eyes clouded with confusion, as if she were asking herself: But how would that work?

Seeing her mom struggle made Kimiko feel sort of sorry for her, as though her mom were the child and she were the adult.

"It'll be okay, Mom. Really it will. You'll see."

Her mom raised an eyebrow, with an expression that was either hopeful or skeptical. "Do you really think so?"

"Yeah, Mom." Kimiko couldn't believe how confident her voice sounded. "I really do."

Her mom held Kimiko's gaze and at last said, "I'm sorry."

It was the first time in a long while that Kimiko could remember her mom apologizing. The fire seemed to be draining out of the dragon.

"It's okay," Kimiko said.

Her mom nodded and glanced at Kimiko's leather jacket. "Are you going out?"

"Yeah, later," Kimiko said, no longer in a rush to leave. "I'm going with Sergio to meet Allie and another friend."

"How is Allie doing?" her mom asked. Her tone seemed to lighten a little. "You haven't invited her over lately."

"She's fine," Kimiko said and noticed her mom's face turn pensive again.

"Is she . . ." Her mom's voice wavered as she seemed to grapple for the right words, ". . . a special friend?"

Kimiko wasn't sure how to answer. "I think she is." But they still had to sort it out. "I hope so."

"Well, I hope so, too," her mom said and stood up. She gave Kimiko a tiny smile. Kimiko smiled back, relieved that their impasse was over. Her mom opened her arms and leaned toward Kimiko, giving her a tender hug. It surprised Kimiko; hugging wasn't something her mom did very often. And Kimiko hugged her in return.

"Thanks, Mom," she whispered and felt her mom's body quiver.

"Just be careful, promise?" her mom said. And the tears flowed, from both of them.

After lunch Kimiko walked the three blocks to Sergio's house, shaking out her arms along the way.

"Do I look all right?" she asked as they drove together to the mall.

"Love the shirt." He grinned. It was one of his—or it used to be. "You look mighty fine. What about me?"

He was having his own jitters. It felt as if he were meeting Lance for the first time all over again.

Kimiko reached across the car seat and dabbed an eyelash off his cheek. "There. Now you're perfect."

"Yeah, right." He turned in to the mall parking lot, pulled into a space, and shut the engine off. But then they both just sat there. Unmoving. Neither of them getting out.

"Ready, dude?" Her voice quavered a little.

"Yeah." He reached over and grabbed her hand. "Are you?"

"Yeah." She squeezed his hand in return. It felt as sweaty as her own.

"Come on, we can do this," he told her. "At the count of three. Okay? One, two, three!"

Simultaneously, they unclasped hands and threw open their doors.

Sergio examined his reflection in about a hundred store windows as they walked toward the food court. But when he spotted Lance, all of his nervousness seemed to slip away. He was fully ready to try it with Lance again, stepping into it with both feet this time.

"Hi," Lance said, smiling wider than he'd ever smiled in his life.

As they began to talk, it felt as if they'd never broken up. And even though Lance tried hard not to get ahead of himself, he hoped they'd never break up again.

"My mom says hi," Kimiko told Allie while the boys caught up. "She's talking to me again—finally!"

"Oh, gosh, that's great!" Allie said with a giggle. She felt so happy to see Kimiko—more than just happy, all fluttery inside.

"Yeah," Kimiko continued. "I think she finally gets that I'm not a lesbian to defy her or punish her or anything. She even apologized."

"Wow," Allie said. "No more Dragon Lady?"

"She's gone into her cave." Kimiko giggled. "Hey, why is it that I always get the giggles when I'm with you?"

"I don't know." Allie giggled too, again. "Am I that funny looking?"

"No," Kimiko said and her face added: *Hardly*.

"Sergio and I are going to get smoothies," Lance said to them. "Or maybe some eats. Do you guys want to get something?"

Allie turned to Kimiko. "Are you hungry? What would you like to do?"

"Dude, I'm stuffed." Kimiko patted her stomach. "My mom made this huge lunch—because she felt guilty, I guess. And I ate it because *I* felt guilty. But if you're hungry . . ." She remembered their *Girl Panic* routine. "I'll buy you doughnuts. Just don't blame me if you get fat!"

"Yes, buy me doughnuts!" Allie giggled and clapped her hands. "No, I'm kidding. I already ate. Hey, you want to drive around and listen to music and go somewhere? It's a beautiful day."

"Sure!" Kimiko said. She'd dreamed of riding in Allie's car again.

They left the boys, kidding them to "Behave!" and went out to the parking lot. It truly was a gorgeous day. The sun was bright but the air was cool, perfect for rolling down the glass and singing out the windows. The autumn leaves swirled in the breeze outside. And a little red daisy sat in the dashboard vase.

Allie drove to a park down by the river where they sat and talked about manga and karate and math puzzles and the musical that Lance wanted her to audition for with him. She felt so good to be with Kimiko again. It didn't matter whether they were just friends or might eventually possibly be more than that. She liked being with her.

"Oh, before I forget . . ." she told Kimiko and pulled a folded page from beside the gearshift. "I found this under the seat. I guess it fell out of your pocket."

It was Kimiko's poem from the last time they'd been together . . . When they'd kissed.

"You can keep it," Kimiko told her. "If you want."

"Really? Yeah, of course. Thanks!" She touched the page to her chest for an instant. That was kind of dramatic, but she meant it.

And as they sat watching some kids fly a rainbow-color kite, Kimiko worked up the nerve for what she most wanted to talk about.

"So, you told me you broke up with Chip. How is that going?"

"Okay," Allie said, glad that Kimiko had brought it up. "It's a little bit weird at lunch, since we all sit together, but I'm dealing. He hasn't told anybody yet, which is good. I mean, everybody knows we broke up, but he hasn't told them about . . . you know . . . the bi stuff."

"So, do you still think you might be bi?" Kimiko asked, swallowing the baseball-sized lump in her throat.

"Yeah," Allie answered, swallowing the knot in her own throat. "I don't know for sure . . . But . . ." She took a deep breath and let it out again, "I keep thinking about . . . when we kissed."

She gazed across the car at Kimiko. Kimiko looked away. She had to; she felt so nervous.

"Me too," she said, certain she'd turned as red as the daisy in the dashboard vase. She had to force herself to look into Allie's eyes. "I'm scared, dude."

Allie responded with a little nod. "I'm scared too."

"Really?" Kimiko asked. "But you've got all this

experience, you're beautiful, self-confident . . ."

"I don't know about the beautiful," Allie said, "or the confident. And as for the experience I have, it's with guys. You're the first girl . . . This is all brand-new to me. It feels so different from being with a guy. But . . ." Her heart caromed against her chest. "I know I liked kissing you."

"I liked kissing you, too," Kimiko said. Her gaze shifted from Allie's eyes to her lips. She wished Allie would kiss her again. Right this instant.

"But," Allie continued, "if you don't think it can work between us, then I'm fine with us being friends. I respect that. It's fine. Most of all, I just like being with you. Whatever we are is fine."

The triple *fine* made Kimiko think it was totally *not* fine. Every word Allie said was only making Kimiko want her more.

"So, what are we going to do?" Kimiko asked, as doubts and insecurities whirled around inside her head.

"I don't know," Allie said. She pulled the red daisy out of the dashboard vase and handed it to Kimiko. "What do you want to do?"

Kimiko brought the flower up to her nose and took in the scent. Then she twirled it in her fingers. She figured they could probably talk and talk about this for weeks, and hopefully that would help them make up their minds . . . or . . .

She leaned forward a little, watching Allie's lips. Allie did the same, bending toward Kimiko's mouth. In the kiss that followed, all of Kimiko's doubts and uncertainties melted away. And in her mind she heard Sergio cheering, "Yee-hah!"

They kissed, then watched the rainbow-striped kite soar over the river. And Allie thought for a moment how she could hardly wait to tell Lance the news. Then she and Kimiko kissed some more.

ABOUT THE AUTHOR

Alex Sanchez received his master's degree in guidance and counseling from Old Dominion University, and worked for many years as a youth and family counselor. His novels include the Lambda Award–winning *So Hard to Say*, the Rainbow Boys trilogy, and *Bait*. When not writing, Alex tours the country talking with teens, librarians, and educators about the importance of teaching tolerance and self-acceptance. Originally from Mexico, Alex now lives in Thailand and Hollywood, Florida. Visit Alex at AlexSanchez.com.